Still
Quiet As
Kept

Vincent
McDaniels

Copyright ©2020 by Vincent McDaniels
ISBN 978-0-578-75678-3

Visit HELIMITE.COM to contact the author.

Cover art: NEENALOVE Inc.
Elements of Cover Art sourced from artists on
123rf.com - poemsuk kinchokawat

This book is dedicated to my mother, Apostle Dorothy M. Fairbanks.

Momma, I wish that you were here to see all that I have done.
I love and miss you so much.
You would be so proud of your son.
Rest in Heaven.

Still Quiet As Kept

Acknowledgements

I would like to thank, first and foremost, my Heavenly Father for blessing me with the ability to express myself on paper and for giving me an awesome editor, in Jesus' name. Amen.

To my family: I love you all. Thank you for your support, advice, and patience.

A special thank you to: Windy Hill, Zully Hicks, Nadine Neal, Avis Chapman Reese, Alyson Harris, Veleka Kearse, Stacye Anderson, LaShanda Smith, and Clarissa Greenwood.
These soul sisters not only embraced my first book into their book clubs but bugged the hell out of me to finish part two.

Special Thank You to my power line family: Alfred (Dog), Jeff (Vince get a 6-pack), Hood (thas whassup), Hollywood (thanks for sending me home), D.J. (whassup my guy), Victor (Yooo my brother), Cuz (my brother), Big Mike (Das on me baby), Lil-D (home team), Sam (Landlord), Red (chasing the bag), T. John (my brother), Downtown Brown (where it all began), No Neck (not going to the strip club, man), Harper (you gon lift all the weights?), Paul Lance (7 on that), Mark (good brother), Javie (keep ya head up).

This book could have and would have been finished months ago but my editor, Neena Love, fell head over heels in love and lost her appetite and her mind! LOL

Last but not least, a special thank you to everyone who has ever prayed for me, pointed me in the right direction, encouraged me, and constantly reminded me that God has a plan for me.

Still Quiet As Kept

1

"I thought I said absolutely no smoking on this bus,"
the Transport Officer screamed over the intercom.

I'm sitting at the back of the bus, alone, with shackles
on my feet, wondering what prison I was being delivered to.
I am in deep thought looking at all the graffiti and drawings
written into the walls of this bus. Every city, every county,
and every nickname in the state of Florida has left its

signature on these seats and walls. Hitman from Miami Florida. Big Boss Fluff from 561. Orange Man Dade County. Duck Fort Lauderdale. Pana Cat slid thru hea 1991. There are so many names and places covering the walls and seats, people that I might see and places that I will never see in the foreseeable future.

It is still hard to believe that I left Polk C.I. It is going to be a while before I get over the fact that I will never see Ms. Washington or Coach Willis again unless the Fourth District Court of Appeals overturns my case and sets me free. I am so glad GQ encouraged me to "seize the moment" with Ms. Washington. If I had more time, I could have established something more significant with Coach Willis as well.

It is apparent that Coach Willis isn't as low key as she thinks she is because Inspector Bradley has her on his radar. I still can't believe how Inspector Bradley tried to persuade me into becoming an informant for him. The way I see it, everybody has to eat and I would never be the reason for taking food out of anyone's mouth.

"If I smell one more cigarette, I'm going to pull this bus over and slap the shit outta somebody," the Transport Officer shouts!

He continues, "Y'all can smoke once we arrive at Hardee Correctional Institution."

Hardee is just forty-five minutes away from Polk C.I. The bus is only half full. I can hear other inmates asking questions. No one had any information about Hardee C.I. because it was a brand-new prison located in Bowling Green, Florida. I don't know what to expect when I arrive there. All I know is what I was taught at Polk C.I. If it don't make money, it don't make sense. I have twenty-three hundred dollars and one ounce of weed stashed inside of my Super 2 radio.

I am looking out the window of the bus, through the steel cage, at the woods and the cows grazing in the fields.

An overwhelming smell of a dead animal takes over the bus. Inmates start moving as fast as they can, with shackles on, to other empty seats.

The Transport Officer screams, "Whoever just farted needs some bleach poured down their asshole. Y'all fire them cigarettes up ASAP."

I couldn't stop laughing at the scene playing out in front of me. Thirty minutes later, the bus pulls into the Sally Port Gate at Hardee C.I. About fifteen officers come out to meet the bus with three nurses and two Classification Officers.

A lieutenant with a clipboard steps inside the bus and shouts, "When I call your name, give me your DC number and get off the bus. Inmate Helimite!"

The lieutenant was about 5'10" wearing his white Department of Correction's shirt, buttoned all the way up with a brown tie on. His shirt and pants were so tight, I am pretty sure it was hard for him to breathe. He wore a cowboy style Department of Correction's hat and he used the word, "Boy" or "Boys" in every other sentence, which were clear signals that he was a redneck.

I respond, "182454, sir." This DC number in the prison system is more important than your actual name. It is a unique number issued to every single inmate when you enter the Department of Corrections.

I grab all my property and get off the bus. The officers instruct me to face the wall while they unshackle me. I lift each leg, one at a time as they remove the shackles from my ankles. They instruct me to turn around to face the officer as he removes the handcuffs from my wrists. The rest of the inmates exit the bus in similar fashion and are unshackled and uncuffed in the same way. I am so happy to have these shackles off my ankles. They were put on so tight that it left an imprint in the skin around my ankles.

Every inmate is lined up, nose to the wall, with their property at their feet. The lieutenant is the last to get off the bus. He is pacing behind us and shouts, "I don't care about what prison you came from, you will answer every staff member here 'yes sir, no sir, yes ma'am, no ma'am.' Do you understand?"

"Yes sir," we sound off in unison.

The Lieutenant directs Sergeant Chew to escort us to the visitation park. Sergeant Chew is tall and lanky with a tennis ball amount of chewing tobacco in his right cheek. He spews out a wad of tobacco juice onto the grass and says with a heavy back wood accent, "Y'all boys heard the boss. Grab your property. Get in a single file line and head toward that there visitation park."

We line up, single file, and are escorted to the visitation park to be processed. The intake process is the same as it was at Polk C.I. We are strip-searched, our property is searched, and we are given a haircut before they escort us to the Medical Department.

As I stand here looking at this compound, all I can say is, "Damn, I'm in a real prison now!" Polk C.I., the prison I just left, looked like a college campus compared to this place. At Polk C.I., there were trees, flowers, and pigeons everywhere and a well-kept landscape of green grass that we played football on every time it rained. It was against the rules to play football due to all the injuries it caused but when it rained the officers would not come out to stop us. C-Dorm, also known as the Castle versus D-Dorm, also known as the Dog House was some of the most violent, bone-crushing football games you would ever see. No pads. No helmets.

"Inmate Helimite get in line," a Corrections Officer shouted, interrupting my memory of Polk C.I.

"If you all have any medical passes get them out for the nurse and doctors to review."

I'm hot as fish grease, still, at how I was transferred so quickly to Hardee C.I. This prison was brand new. There are six dormitories, all two-man cells. No basketball courts. No weights. There was one pull up bar, one dip bar, and a softball field. Overcrowding in the prison system is so bad in Florida that every county had built or were in the process of building a prison.

"Dr. Smith, how you doing sir?" I look up to see Inmate Gene addressing the doctor like they had some history together.

"Inmate Gene! What are you doing here?" Dr. Smith asks.

Inmate Gene replies, "I put in for a good adjustment transfer to Lake C.I. and was sent here instead. Do you have any positions available for medical orderlies?"

"I sure do. I need at least two orderlies to strip wax and buff these floors up here on a regular basis."

"Well, Dr. Smith, you know I have experience in everything that you mentioned and I have a good friend who is familiar with that type of work as well."

Dr. Smith answers Inmate Gene, "Write down your names and DC numbers and I'll submit the names to classification tomorrow."

"No problem. Thank you, sir," Inmate Gene says as Dr. Smith walks off, barking out orders to the nurses to speed up the intake process with all the new arrivals.

I tap Inmate Gene on the arm and ask, "Bro, where you know Dr. Smith from?"

Inmate Gene explains that Dr. Smith was the doctor at Polk C.I. for four years and that he quit two months ago and came to Hardee C.I. for more money. Inmate Gene was a medical orderly at Polk C.I. for years. Whenever I needed to buy alcohol pads or peroxide or calamine lotion for my shaving bumps, I went to Inmate Gene. He was a cool brother with a mouth full of silver-capped teeth.

I never met a brother who carried a brush with him at all times the way that Inmate Gene did. I take that back. I attended North Shore High School and we were nicknamed the "pretty-boy high school." All the guys wore *Polo* brand clothing. The majority of my classmates kept a brush with them at all times to keep the wave patterns in their hair in place. I can still see Bowly, Sam, Bullet Head Tim, and the Jeter brothers brushing their hair constantly. In class. In between classes. In the hallways. Walking around campus. Me, on the other hand, had a bad grade of hair and I kept my hair as low cut to my scalp as possible.

Inmate Gene is from St. Petersburg, Florida. He is a *quiet as kept* convict even though the Department of Corrections addressed us all as inmates. It didn't matter though because everyone doing time knew who all the convicts were. A convict is a seasoned veteran at doing time and an inmate was still new to the system trying to figure everything out.

"Hey Gene, I overheard Dr. Smith say he needs two orderlies. Can you hook me up with that other available position?"

Inmate Gene looked at me and said, "For the right price, Helimite, I can make it happen."

"What's your price?" I ask.

"Twenty-five dollars and you got the job," he snaps back.

"Well I guess I'm in then. I'll give you the twenty-five once we get to whatever dorm they putting us in."

Inmate Gene nods in agreement and asks me if I have ever stripped, waxed or buffed floors before.

I tell him quickly, "Hell naw but I'm a quick learner!"

He laughs and shakes my hand. "Write your name and DC number down so I can turn it in to Dr. Smith."

After almost two hours of waiting to be seen by the medical staff we all leave and head toward the kitchen for lunch. There are hardly any inmates moving around the prison, which leads me to believe that this prison must be on lock down for something. The prison can be locked down for a number of reasons including attempted escape or a stabbing. In a lockdown there is no movement. Inmates are confined to their cell. I grab a tray and make my way through the chow line. I don't recognize anyone at all. I sit down and start to eat the hamburger and grilled potatoes. It is good and hot.

I ask one of the kitchen workers, "Where everybody at?"

He replies, "What you mean?"

I said, "The rest of the inmates. Where they at?"

He laughs and says, "Bro, it's only about 200 inmates at this prison right now. Well 235 now since you all arrived today. All them dorms you see are empty except for Dorm One. Dorm one is halfway full. I'm pretty sure you all will be housed there as well."

I shake my head in anger and curse under my breath. I left Polk by force not by choice and the offer the Inspector presented to me was out of the question. Setting someone up or snitching on any illegal activity I may have knowledge of isn't the route I was taught to take. No one has a clue as to why and what purpose the illegal activity is serving. The staff member could be struggling to pay rent, pay a car note, feed their children, or any other household expenses. Different strokes for different folks. I choose to stay *quiet as kept*, which is a rare trait in this day and age. At the same time, once the word is out that you're a snitch your days have just become numbered.

2

Housing One, Quad Three, Room 207 is my assigned place of residence at Hardee C.I. The room had never been lived in before. The mattress and the pillow still had the new plastic seal over it. My roommate, a brother named Hollywood from Miami who hadn't said three words since we arrived at Hardee, was assigned the bottom bunk since he was older than me. Hollywood had a pair of Blues Brother shades that he wore all the time. You never knew where he was actually looking because the shades were so dark. He was about 5'7", 170 pounds and rarely spoke a word. I automatically thought he was slow or may have ridden the short yellow bus. For the most part, as long as he respected me and cleaned up behind himself we would get along just fine.

Just like *L.L. Cool J*, I couldn't live without my radio. My radio talks to me, sings to me, raps to me, and puts me to sleep every single night. My radio is the size of a cereal box. It has one big speaker and a tweeter. It is AM-FM only. More importantly, my radio is also my mobile, secure stash spot. I have a pair of finger nail clippers that I had filed down to a screwdriver shape to be able to go inside my radio whenever I needed to.

I transferred to Hardee with one ounce of that good, light green weed, with the red hairs in it, and 23 one hundred-dollar bills. They were in a plastic bag, taped to the back of the circuit board of the radio. My plan is to access my stash spot after the 11 p.m. lights out call and after Hollywood is sound asleep. I dump all my property on my bunk. I had ten bars of Dove soap, eight speed stick deodorant, and enough cans of tuna and boxes of club house crackers to feed twenty people, a jar of peanut butter, and a bottle of honey.

I was organizing my locker when the dorm intercom blasts, "Five minutes 'til four p.m. count. All inmates report to your bunk for count and secure your doors."

I grab my drinking cup and head down stairs to the water fountain to fix me a cup of *Tang* to drink while I wait on count to clear. It shouldn't take long with only 235 inmates here. I tune my radio to an AM station called 1380 The Touch. A new R&B group named *Mint Condition* was on the radio with their new hit single, *Pretty Brown Eyes*. It sounded exactly like a hit to me. I lay back and try to remember if I even knew a female with pretty brown eyes.

As I go down memory lane I can recall only one girl with pretty brown eyes. Her name was Cheryl also known as Sweetie. She had a younger sister named Sabrina. These two sisters were divas at John F. Kennedy Jr. High School and probably didn't even know it.

I'll never forget the day my best friend Teddy Donald told me he was dating Sabrina. I put down the cane pole I was fishing with and said, "You lying, Joker!"

He laughed and said, "I got the Midas touch, Helimite."

Teddy and I have known each other since Lincoln Elementary School. We became fast friends through our love of fishing and pretty girls.

The intercom sounded off once again, "Count time. All inmates must be sitting in an upright position facing the wall."

I turn my radio all the way down and sit up and face the wall. My roommate does the same. Two officers walk by one at a time looking through the window. Once they finish counting, an officer yells out, "Relax!" It is an indication that I can lie back down and continue whatever it was that I was doing. Ten minutes later the count is complete and the loud clicking sound of doors being unlocked breaks the silence.

The intercom sounds off, "If you are going to chow, line up. You must be clean shaven unless you have a shaving pass that allows you to have a beard."

I line up and head to the chow hall that is about sixty yards away. The menu reads Fish and Grits for dinner. I wasn't about to miss that. The kitchen workers are piling the food on the trays. The pieces of catfish are as long as the tray and served with two scoops of grits. I know this good eating isn't going to last forever. The more inmates arrive here to fill all these empty dorms up, the smaller the portions will get. I sit down at a table with three other guys that are strangers to me. There's a bottle of hot sauce and salt and pepper on every table in the kitchen. Up against the wall there is a huge clear dispenser filled with, what appears to be, grape *Kool Aid*.

I eat my food like I am starving because three, young White officers are screaming at us that we have ten minutes to finish our meal. I doubt that was a rule but I wasn't about to challenge these officer's authority. I have bigger things to deal with like trying to find change for a hundred-dollar bill to pay Inmate Gene the twenty-five dollars to secure the medical orderly job.

As I put my empty tray in the tray window to be washed, one of the young officers singles me out. I give him the nickname Vanilla Ice because of his faded-up haircut and expensive looking shades.

"Inmate Helimite, turn around and put your hands on top of your head."

I asked, "What for?"

Vanilla Ice screams, "Because I gave you an order to!"

I do as he directs. He pats me down from my shoulders to my ankles.

"Okay Inmate Helimite. You're good."

I turn to face him and ask, "Sir, what were you searching for?"

He points to a table nearby where five bottles of hot sauce are. I shake my head and walk out of the dining hall.

As I exit the dining hall, I walk toward the north end of the prison to get a spot in the rotation. The inmates have already established a routine on the only dip bar and pull-up bar at this prison.

I walk up and shout out, "Who the last man on the dip bar?"

Somebody hollers, "I am, Stonybrook!"

I turn and look to my left to see who was addressing me by my home turf name, Stonybrook. To my surprise it's one of my homeboys, Dr. Rock, from the Ivey Green housing complex in Riviera Beach, Florida. I walk up to him and give him a hand shake and a brotherly hug. We exchange small talk and I ask him what he's been up to. He tells me that he has been at Hardee for a month and was a part of the first one hundred people at Hardee C.I.

I fire off a round of questions. "Are there any Black people that work here?"

"It's a few. Ten, at the most," Dr. Rock replies.

"Any females?"

Dr. Rock quickly responds, "Six. I've counted six so far."

"How many brothers here from Palm Beach?"

"Three. Me, you, and Nardo."

To be clear and be sure I heard Dr. Rock correctly I repeat, "Nardo?"

Nardo was from Federal Gardens in Riviera Beach. He played football at Suncoast High alongside N.F.L. superstar wide-receiver Anthony Carter. I often saw Nardo at Jiffy Store wheeling and dealing. He always wore a thick Run DMC gold chain. I never actually saw him play football but he was built like a tank and was blacker than the prison boots I had on. Nardo was at least 5'10", 250 pounds.

Dr. Rock was around 5'11", 230 pounds. I went to school with Dr. Rock's younger brother, Tiffon. Whenever Stonybrook played against Ivey Green in basketball or football, Dr. Rock was always around to prevent us from fighting. Of course, Stonybrook always won the basketball and football games because that's what we did all day with our free time – we played ball!

The Rec yard was covered in cow manure and the flies never stopped buzzing.

"Helimite, it's your turn," Dr. Rock says.

I jump up to the pull-up bar and do ten reps, walk a few feet away and position myself on the dip bar and do ten reps. When I get off the dip bar, I notice Nardo talking to Dr. Rock. I am certain that Dr. Rock is informing Nardo about me, who I was, what I was in prison for, and what part of Palm Beach County I was from.

I walk toward their direction.

Nardo shouts, "I don't wanna talk, Dr. Rock. I'm here to get thick and get myself in better shape and we can't achieve that talking."

Dr. Rock laughs and says, "Helimite, we normally do one hundred dips, a hundred pull ups and two hundred push-ups every evening. You welcome to ride with us."

I agree.

"Nardo, what's up brother?" I say.

Nardo responds, "Nothing but all this time the White man done gave us."

I nod my head in agreement.

Dr. Rock says, "Nardo, save all that conversation and get a set in. Helimite, you can start the push up rotation. We do twenty-five a set."

I drop down and start my push-ups while listening to a new rap group, *The Geto Boys'* hit song *My Mind is Playing Tricks on Me.*

At night I can't sleep, I toss and turn

Candlesticks in the dark, visions of bodies being burned

Four walls just staring at a nigga

I'm paranoid, sleeping with my finger on the trigger

Nardo stops me mid push-up and says, "Helimite, it's twenty-five push-ups on your knuckles, not your hands. We hit hard in Riviera Beach and to ensure that, we do push-ups on our knuckles, brother."

I nod my head and do the twenty-five push-ups on my knuckles. It is somewhat painful but I wasn't about to complain. There's an old saying in the prison system, No Pain No Gain! We finish our work out and head to the canteen, which is the prison version of *7-11*. We buy three jungle juices and walk away from everyone else, toward the softball field.

I ask Dr. Rock where he worked. He proudly explains that he is the Staff Canteen Man and Visiting Park

Canteen man. I have to admit that Dr. Rock had a sweet job. He not only saw all the staff and was able to interact with them at the Staff Canteen, on the weekends he saw and interacted with every visitor who came to see an inmate at the Visiting Park Canteen.

I ask Nardo where he worked. He describes his job as the Inside Grounds Clerk. He issues out the rakes, brooms, shovels and whatever else that is needed to keep the Hardee C.I. landscape clean.

"I have a small office next to the barbershop," Nardo finishes.

I chime in, "My next four days will be spent in Hardee C.I. orientation class but I'm pretty sure I have a job starting in the Medical Department on Monday."

"Good luck with that," Dr. Rock sighs. "Ain't no way they gonna assign your Black ass to Medical Department with all them White women up in there."

I shrug, "I guess you right but you never know."

I continue, "I got a question to ask you brother. I always was curious about how you obtained the nickname Dr. Rock."

He laughs and explains that the women in Palm Beach County gave him that nickname.

"It's due to me curing all their aches and pains when they get with me. I'm just like Marvin Gaye, Helimite. I provide Sexual Healing!"

Nardo and I start laughing.

Nardo tells Dr. Rock, "You have to carry an asthma pump with you to keep up with the ladies."

Dr. Rock fires back, "I keep my asthma pump with me like a preacher carries the Bible."

As Dr. Rock is saying this, he pulls an asthma pump out of his front pocket and hits it twice.

"Bing! Bing! Bing! The doctor is ready for whatever!"

As if on cue, the prison P.A. system came alive and announced, "Attention on the compound. Inmate Rock, report to the Staff Canteen immediately."

I tell Rock, "Since you so ready for whatever, go serve them donuts, sodas, sandwiches and chips to the officers"

He smiles at me and responds, "They pay me seventy-five dollars a month to work in that canteen so I serve them up with a smile!"

He gives Nardo and I some dap and leaves us to do two hundred jumping jacks in silence.

3

Nardo asks me, "You from Stonybrook, right?"

I nod, affirmative.

He continues, "I had a girlfriend named Cookie who used to live over there. Y'all had some wild young brothers livin' over there and some of the finest females in Riviera Beach as well. Y'all had brothers scared to come up in Stonybrook."

I answer, "Yeah. It's one way in and one way out of Stonybrook and you better be on your best behavior up in there or get beat up."

"Man Helimite, times have really changed in Palm Beach County," Nardo explains. "There was a time when you could have a fist fight with anybody and shake hands and be back friends in no time at all. The worst-case scenario was you used a stick or some brass knuckles to hit somebody with but now it's all about the gun play."

Nardo continues, "Everybody has a gun now. How all these guns got into the community is beyond me. How old are you, Helimite?"

I turned twenty-one on my last birthday. Most twenty-one year olds are graduating from college or working and figuring life out. It would have been nice to be in free society and be able to walk into a store and purchase my first bottle of liquor but instead, I'm here on the inside having to settle for prison wine.

"And you been locked up for how long?" Nardo asks.

"Since I was seventeen."

Nardo raises an eyebrow. "What pushed you into this gangster lifestyle of gun slinging in Palm Beach County, brother?"

I go into deep thought as I recall that life-altering event that took place on July 6th, 1985. I was fifteen years old. Myself, Vell, Bake Bean, Charlie Wine, Blow Pop, Bowly, Jeff and Kurt Rawls piled into three different cars. There's a gray and black *Monte Carlo*. Kurt had a four door *Buick LeSabre* and my Aunt Pearl had a two door, all white *Mercury Cougar*. We had to beg Aunt Pearl and give her cash to use her *Mercury Cougar* for the night. She had two conditions for using the car. The first was that we were not allowed to take her car to Trail Skateway. The second condition was that the gas tank needed to be full when we returned it.

We headed to West Palm Beach to see if anything was happening at Gaines Park. We were disappointed when we got there because it was dead empty. We parked as some of the fellows smoked a few joints of that Columbian Gold weed. I didn't smoke back then because I had heard that it killed your brain cells. I knew that I wasn't the sharpest dude especially in math class so I skipped the weed and only drank beer. Vell knew that and always made sure I had a quart of Private Stock.

I pop the top on my beer and take a good swig.

"Y'all know Gaines Park only be jumping on Sundays! Today is Saturday. Trail Skateway is where everybody is tonight. I know Aunt Pearl don't want her car over there but all we doing is riding through. We not going in."

I say it as convincing as possible and continue, "Y'all got any guns with y'all in case any of them brothers from the White House housing project wanna try us?"

Kurt answers, "I got a 12-gauge shot gun behind the back seat."

Charlie Wine pulls out his old faithful .22 handgun. A gun he stole out of someone's truck one day while we were fishing.

"Let's ride y'all," I say as I jump in the front seat of the *Monte Carlo* and turn up the volume.

Run DMC is playing on the car's cassette player.

Together Forever. Forever Together.

Run DMC and we're tougher than leather.

We makin' and breakin' and scratchin' and taking.

To be fo' real, we could never be faking.

Everybody in the car is rapping along with the beat. We were headed down Australian Ave toward 45th Street when Charlie Wine shouts over the loud music, "I'm hungry. Stop by Pizza Hut, the Stonybrook Hut."

On the street, everyone called it the Stonybrook Hut because if thirty people worked there, twenty-eight of them lived in Stonybrook. So, once we crossed 45th Street we made a left into the Pizza Hut parking lot. Our home girls DeeDee and Yolanda were working up front at the cash register. We ordered three large supreme pan pizzas and paid a total of ten dollars. DeeDee and Yolanda would never charge us full price for anything. We waited twenty minutes for the pizzas to get done. We played Donkey Kong and Ms. Pac Man video games in the lobby while we waited. Those three pizzas between the eight of us didn't last long due to everyone but me having the munchies from the weed.

We jump back into the cars and head toward Trail Skateway. We are riding and jamming to *You Got a Big Mouth* by *Whodini*. It takes about fifteen minutes to arrive at Trail Skateway and when I say there was nowhere to park, it was sold out. The new rap group out of Miami, *2 Live Crew*, was performing in there and you could feel the bass bumping outside in the parking lot. *Jump! Jump! Jump! Jump!*

Everybody ghetto Jump! Man, the whole Palm Beach County is up in there doing the *Ghetto Jump*.

Vell says, "Man we should have bought some tickets."

I'm like, "Yeah, but we hadn't planned to come. Wait a minute Vell. Pull over. That looks like Kooley C over there smoking a joint."

I jump out the car and shout, "Kooley C. Wassup homie?"

"Hey Helimite," Kooley C gives me a hug and tries to pass me the joint.

I tell him I'm good and he says, "You and my brother Russell are the only two negros I know that don't smoke weed."

I laugh and say, "Me and my homeboys need to get up in there. It's eight of us total."

Kooley C responds, "Walk in with me and we will open the side door to let the rest of the crew in."

"Bet," I say. "Let me go tell the rest of the fellas what the plan is so they can park somewhere and be on point to come in through the side door."

Kooley C keeps smoking his joint and coughing between each pull. We parked in a field across the street from the Trail Skateway. I walk through the front door with Kooley C. The person taking the tickets at the booth didn't question anything because Kooley C and KJ deejayed there every weekend. The lights were dim. It was standing room only. The disco lights were blinking everywhere and whoever invented these new stretch pants all the girls seem to be wearing could surely get my vote as Designer of the Year.

2 Live Crew was taking a break and KJ was spinning *Egyptian Lover.*

Egypt is the place to be. Egypt! Egypt!

Palm Beach County was popping and locking, stomping and grinding. All I can do is smile because as soon as we open this side door and Charlie Wine hits the dance floor, he will transform into a dancing machine. It is much darker against the wall of the dance floor where all the wanna-be gangsters and players were posted watching all the movement. Kooley C and I open the side door all the way in the back, which really is a fire exit.

The Stonybrook crew stepped in there like they owned the building. The gangsters and players that are posted against the wall gave us the head nod of respect and we kept it moving. I spotted a sexy lil tenderoni that went to Palm Beach Gardens High School. I was trying to remember her name as I walked over to her. She was standing by the concession window when I approached her.

"Hey pretty lady. Why you over here all by yourself?" I ask.

She turns and looks at me and says, with her hands on her hips, "I'm waiting on a hot dog."

I tell her, "Baby you might as well let me order us a cheeseburger and some fries and let me explain to you why I'm so interested in you and hopefully we can exchange the seven digits."

She burst out laughing and I'm thinking to myself, did I say something funny or corny.

The music was so loud. KJ was playing some jam called *I Wonder If I Take You Home* by *Lisa Lisa*. I reached for the girl's hand and ask, "You wanna dance?"

She snatches her hand away and says something again about a hot dog.

I shake my head and say, "You must be really hungry."

Before she could respond, a little, short, swol' brother who looks like he just got out of prison grabs her by the arm and asks her, "Why you disrespecting me talking to this negro?"

She shouts over the music, "I told him I was waiting on you, Hotdog!"

I'm like, oh shit, her boyfriend's name is Hotdog. I'm already sizing up how this fight is going to play out. I'm taller than him with longer arms so I wasn't going to let this short swol' brother named Hotdog grab me. It was going to be all knuckles to the head. There's no way I was going to explain to this brother that I thought his girlfriend had said she ordered a hot dog. I wasn't about to cop a plea and appear to be scared or soft.

Hotdog looks at me and says, "Punk mother fucker, you won't never dis' me again," and grabs the girl and leaves. I later find out that the girl's name was Nicole Mason.

I let out a sigh of relief and head back to the wall where the Stonybrook crew is posted. Just as I expected, Charlie Wine had a circle of people surrounding him as he danced to *Doug E. Fresh*'s hit song, *The Show*. I can still hear the lyrics.

Excuse me Doug E Fresh

Yes?

Have you ever seen a show with fellas on the mic

With one minute rhymes that don't come out right

They bite, they never write, that's not polite

Am I lying?

No, you're quite right

I'm against the wall now bobbing my head to the beat wishing I knew how to dance like Charlie Wine. Skinny Legs, my classmate from the Federal Gardens neighborhood, approaches me and says, "Helimite. I don't know what's going on but I overheard Hotdog say that you better not be here when he get back."

I tell Skinny Legs, "Fuck Hotdog. I'm a Cheeseburger, negro."

We both laugh but, in my spirit, I feel something just ain't right. I pull the Stonybrook crew into a huddle and tell them what transpired.

Vell says, "I know Hotdog. He from Riviera Beach. He lives in the Goodmark Park area off of S Avenue."

Being that we were both from Riviera Beach and we knew where he lived, we really didn't give the Hot Dog situation any more thought.

Before *2 Live Crew* ended their show, we exit out the side door that we entered through. We were trying to beat all the traffic that was on its way out. We pile back in the three cars and head back to Stonybrook. Vell realizes he needs some gas and we have to fill up Aunt Pearl's *Mercury Cougar* as well so we pull into the Amoco Gas station on Blue Heron Boulevard. We jump out, buy sodas and a few cans of potato sticks while Vell pumps the gas. Kurt asks for a couple of snicker bars.

We load the three cars back up and suddenly four cars pull up to the front shoulder of the gas station, which was all dirt and shell rock. The four cars pulled up so fast that it created a thick cloud of dust. Once the dust settled there were at least seven guys holding guns pointed at us. I'm looking at the scene saying to myself that they got all them guns pointed at us just to talk because there's no way they would shoot at us at a gas station and chance blowing some shit up.

Hotdog had a trench coat on and yelled, "What's up now, partner!" as he unloaded a 12-gauge shotgun on all of us in the three cars. The brothers he had with him unloaded their weapons as well. There was no opportunity to fire back at them with the two weapons we possessed. We were overwhelmed and overmatched.

I was screaming like a bitch, "Go! Go! Crank the car and Go!"

The front and side window shattered and glass exploded in every direction. There was so much gunfire my ears were ringing. Vell cranked the car and stepped on the gas and we recklessly jumped back on to Blue Heron Boulevard. We turned right on to North Tech Road until we hit 8th Street, pulled into Stonybrook and jumped out of the car while it was still moving. I bruised myself up and busted my lip during the ride. Blood was everywhere. I just knew one of us was shot or dead. I hadn't heard a single word from anyone, which made me believe even more that somebody was dead.

All of a sudden I hear a woman scream, "Oh my God! My car! Who did this to my car!"

It was my Aunt Pearl.

She warned us not to go to Trail Skateway but we went anyway. Nobody but God saw us through this whole shooting event. He covered us, shielded, and protected us. To see how bad these three cars were shot up and not a single person was shot or dead was God's grace and mercy on full display.

"Nardo, I was shell shocked and angry. All I could think about was revenge! That one night changed my life completely. There was no more fist fighting for me. It was all gunplay now. Shoot first. Ask questions later."

Hotdog would see me again but it would be under much different circumstances.

The prison intercom comes to life and blares out, "Attention on the compound. The yard is now closed. You have ten minutes to report to your dorm for count."

4

I get back to my dorm and take a shower and prepare to write a few letters so everyone knows I have a new address. The first letter I write is to my momma.

Dear Momma,

I pray this letter reaches you in the best of health and spirit. As you can see from the envelope I have been transferred to another prison. It may be thirty minutes closer to Palm Beach. I'm really not sure. I'm gonna call you on Saturday so I can talk to everybody. Teresa wrote me and told me Tanya, Tamia, and Keyna are growing up fast. She also said that Keyna finally stopped sucking her thumb. Teresa also sent some pictures of her baby boy Marquise. I miss y'all so much momma. And I want to apologize again for putting you through all the stress. You raised me right but I wouldn't listen. I was so drawn to them streets even though you told me time and time again that them streets holds nothing but death or prison. You were absolutely right ma. I'll make it outta here one day momma and make you proud of me. I promise. I love you momma. Write back soon not later. I don't need any money. I'm ok. Take care.

Love Your Son,

Vince

P.S. Momma, I'm finally growing a mustache.

I write Ritha, Shorty Brown, Sam, and Tiffany. It really wasn't even a letter. I wrote them more like a note.

Hey. I got moved to a new prison. Here's the address. Take care and send pictures.

I lie back on my bunk and close my eyes and begin to pray.

Father in the name of Jesus, I ask that you keep your hand on me and my family. I thank you for everything you are doing and everything that you're gonna do.

Now I lay down to sleep

I pray to you Lord my soul to keep

If I should die before I wake

I pray to the Lord my soul to take

In Jesus' name. Amen.

I tune my radio to an R&B station that played nothing but slow jams from 10 p.m. to 3 a.m. The last song I remember hearing was *Teenage Love* by Slick Rick before I fell asleep. My roommate, Hollywood, always appeared to have a cold. All the sniffling and blowing his nose never seemed to stop and when he did fall asleep he snored like a grizzly bear. I thank God for my radio and headphones otherwise it would have been a problem.

Even though we were in a two-man room behind a locked door, I still never slept like I did in society. I'm not saying I slept with one eye open but I'm saying that any little noise I heard, I opened my eyes to look things over.

I woke up the next morning to the sound of doors being unlocked from inside the officer's station. I washed up, got dressed, and went downstairs to talk with Inmate Gene about the upcoming NFL playoffs. It didn't take long before the P.A. system sounded off that it was now chow time.

The menu said it was pancakes, oatmeal, and sausage for breakfast. As we lined up to take the walk to the kitchen, it was very important to me to sit with a group of people who were already up way ahead of time for chow. It was because all the inmates running out of their rooms at the last minute didn't stick a toothbrush in their mouth or wash their face. They were the main ones trying to hold a conversation with you. I managed to keep that problem neutralized as much as possible.

We enter the kitchen and I notice they hung quite a few flytraps to kill off the flies that appeared to be holding the kitchen hostage. I ate so fast that the flies never got a chance to land on my plate. Remember you only get ten minutes to eat.

It's an overcast day. You can smell that the rain is not too far away. It really didn't matter though because everyone who arrived on the bus with me had to finish off their last day of orientation. They issued each of us a Hardee

C.I. Handbook and went over it page by page. They had a representative from every department like Medical, Classification, The Chapel, and Recreation, come in and talk with us. Hardee C.I. did not have school or vocational trades available yet. Their main goal was to try and fill all the empty dorms. Once they did that, the state had to supply the prison with more funds due to population growth.

I had already paid Inmate Gene the twenty-five dollars to get me the job in Medical with him. All we were waiting on was the official job sheet from Classification to be posted in the dorm. On Friday, December 13th, 1991 the job sheet read:

Inmate Helimite, New Arrival to Medical Orderly effective immediately.

My boy, Inmate Gene had delivered on his promise. All I had to do now is follow his lead on stripping, waxing, and buffing the floors. I'm happier than a little kid on Christmas morning.

My partner Gigolo used to always tell me back at Polk C.I., "Helimite, if you really miss a woman's touch, you gotta have a job inside the prison working around women. Point blank."

If you are a sexual offender, Classification will never let you work around female staff.

I recall myself responding, "That makes sense, Gigolo. You dead right."

Gigolo answers, "Of course I'm right, Helimite. I'm a gigolo. Remember?"

I can't wait to see the look on Dr. Rock's face this evening when I meet up with him and Nardo for our work out session. They open up the rec yard at 5:30 p.m. and as I am heading to the north end to work out, Inmate Gene calls me. "Hey Helimite! Check this out."

I walk over toward him and give him a handshake and ask, "What's happening Gene?"

He says, "Helimite that job sheet said 'effective immediately.' Let's go see what our work station looks like."

I tell him, "Man, I gotta get my workout in for today."

Inmate Gene responds, "Helimite, look," and points toward the north end.

I see inmates running like the police are chasing them. Behind the inmates was a solid wall of nothing but rain headed our way. At that moment the P.A. system blasted that the yard was closed. "Report back to your dormitories!"

Inmate Gene says, "Follow me."

We approach the Medical Building Officer's station. A white female officer named Mrs. Blake asked us who we were there to see. We advised her that we worked in Medical.

She tilted her pretty little brunette head and asked, "Since when?"

Inmate Gene says, "Today is our first day."

She went to her desk, picked up the job sheet, asked to see our I.D. cards, and popped the door open to let us in. We go through the door. She asks us to wait in the lobby for a minute. We sit down. Another officer comes in and asks us to get against the wall to be pat down and searched. This officer was an African-American man named Brown who we, later on that day, nicknamed Doo Doo Brown because he was a piece of shit!

Doo Doo Brown was about six feet tall and wore his uniform skintight with a tie and the Department of Corrections cowboy styled hat. He was ex-military, from what we heard later on, and was doing everything in his power to make the rank of sergeant. He looked at Inmate Gene and I and asked, "Y'all the new medical orderlies?"

I answered, "Yes, sir!"

He looked us over again and said, "Y'all ain't gonna last. Y'all look like some crooks."

I looked him right in the eyes and said, "Once upon a time, sir, I was a crook but ever since I invited Jesus Christ in my heart, my values and priorities changed."

He looked at me and said, "Get the fuck outta my face with that Christian shit. Y'all commit all them crimes then come to prison and hide behind a Bible. I'm gonna be watching y'all asses so you better stay clean. Do you understand?"

Inmate Gene says, "Yes!"

Doo Doo Brown says, "Wrong answer."

So, I say, "Yes, sir!"

Brown walks off to enter the Medical Officer's Station where the pretty brunette is. She pops the lock to the main entrance door of Medical and Inmate Gene and I walk in. We are greeted by two nurses, Ms. Bracey and Ms. Everrete. The look that was on these two white women's faces spoke volumes. I'm pretty good at reading body language. What I saw in both of these women's eyes was pure shock that they were trying to hide but was failing at it miserably.

Ms. Everette says, "It's good to see that Dr. Smith hired two big strong guys to help situate things in the building. You guys can start by rearranging all the furniture in my nurse's station and then my office."

Ms. Bracey says, "Your names, please?"

We both answer with our names, Inmate Helimite and Inmate Gene. "At your service, ma'am," I joke.

Ms. Bracey says, "Inmate Gene. Dr. Smith mentioned to me that you worked for him at Polk C.I. Welcome aboard guys."

We replied, "Thank you ma'am."

"You guys follow me," Nurse Everette orders.

We enter a nurse's station and it is very clean and tidy. There is a faint smell of bleach. The walls are white with different medical tips and procedures taped to it. There's a scale in the far-left corner, an EKG machine, a gurney pushed up against the wall with a wheelchair next to it, and a picture of a skeleton.

Nurse Everette instructs us to move around examining tables, stock shelves with hydrogen peroxide, rubbing alcohol, pads, and cotton balls.

Nurse Bracey entered the room and asked me if I knew how to make up a bed. I answer her, "Yes, ma'am."

She instructs, "Put on some gloves and follow me."

I grab some gloves and follow her to the back of the Medical Department where the infirmary is located. There are eight beds, a bathtub, and two showers in the infirmary area. Ms. Bracey takes some keys out of her pocket and opens a closet that contained sheets, blankets, and pillowcases. We enter the closet together then she grabs the linen off the shelves and hands them to me. I stood there as she continued to add linen all the way up to my chin.

"We have enough to make up four beds right now," Ms. Bracey says.

She goes to one side of a bed, with me on the other side and we start unfolding sheets and begin tucking in each side. We're putting two sheets and one blanket on each bed with a pillowcase. Once we start on the second bed, Nurse Bracey looks at me and says, "You look and remind me so much of Darrell."

I don't respond. I just listen.

She asks me where I was from.

I tell her, "Palm Beach."

"How old are you?" she asks.

I tell her that I'm 21. I look over at Nurse Bracey as she bends over to grab a blanket and I can see through the white pants she has on. I can clearly see her panty line gripping her ass. She was around 5'7" and was what I would describe as chubby-fine. She had a cute face with brown hair styled in a short bob. She wore bright red lipstick and smoked Virginia Slim cigarettes. She continued on with her questioning. How much time did I have? What did I come to

56

prison for? But her very next question made me go on defense.

Nurse Bracey asked me, "Do you smoke weed?"

I looked right into her glossy blue eyes and say, "No, ma'am. I'm an athlete. I would never put any drugs in my body." I was lying my ass off.

She nodded her head in agreement then once again stated, "You look just like Darrell!"

I said to her, "Nurse Bracey, no disrespect but I hope Darrell looks good."

She responded, "Not only does he look good but he's fine as hell too. He was my boyfriend back in high school."

I'm standing there with a pillowcase in my hand saying to myself, "Boy, it's on like popcorn now. Damn!"

That's when Inmate Gene walks in and says, "Helimite. It's count time. They want me and you to report to the Medical lobby."

We enter the Medical lobby and Officer Doo Doo Brown is waiting on us. He asks what dorm and room we live in. We advise him. He calls in his count to the control room and returns back into the Officer's station with the pretty brunette.

"Can we return back to work, sir?" I ask.

"No you can't, inmate. When count clears I will escort both of you back to your dorms," Officer Doo Doo Brown replies.

Count clears fifteen minutes later.

5

Inmate Gene and I are escorted back to our dorms and as soon as we enter the dorm, all eyes are on us. The other inmates are trying to figure out where the hell we were coming from this time of night. It was none of their business and the code I was living by wouldn't change. I was **STILL QUIET AS KEPT**.

My homeboy Rufus always used to say, "Loose lips sinks ships. These inmates will tell God on Jesus just to transfer closer to home or to get moved to another dorm."

I've learned in a short period of time to never let anything surprise me in this prison system. It's slimy and grimy all in one. I go up to my room, grab a California vegetable soup out of my locker, a can of tuna, and a bag of BBQ corn chips. I add just enough hot water to the soup to cook the noodles. I crush up the BBQ corn chips, open the can of tuna and dump all three into a bowl. I add four packets of mayonnaise and a packet of mustard, and stir. The prison name for this meal is goulash.

I ate this same meal pretty much every night and it was delicious as well as nutritious. I had to keep my weight up and I couldn't depend entirely on the food the kitchen served three times a day. I was weighing close to 218 pounds now. Not being able to lift weights took away from me getting thicker. Pushing and lifting weights bulks your body parts up. Pushups, pull ups, and dips cuts, defines and maintains whatever size you already have.

My roommate Hollywood is in the room with some headphones on. He is constantly sniffling and blowing his nose. This brother has had a cold for quite a while now. I hope it's not contagious. As I reach for my own radio to listen to Orlando's 94.5, I was hoping to receive some mail today but that was a negative. So, I lie there wondering what Beth, my ex-girlfriend, might be up to now.

"Helimite, just write the girl and ask her how she doin'," a voice in my head says.

So, I rise up to get a pen and pad when another voice says, "Helimite, bump Beth. Concentrate on Nurse Bracey! She has given you all the information you need for you to capitalize off of."

I lie back down and say, "You are absolutely right," as if the voice in my head will respond back out loud.

The jam by Michele,

Something in my heart

Something in my heart

Has me hooked on you

is playing in the background so I turn my radio off for two reasons. One, I needed to be a man and get out of my feelings and move on like Beth did. Hell, she was smart. It was simple math to her. I had a fifty-five year sentence. I surely wouldn't wait for her ass if the shoe were on the other foot. And two, I needed to get inside of my radio to get some weed out to smoke for the next day.

Hollywood appeared to be sound asleep so I got out my fingernail clippers/screwdriver and took apart my radio. I took out enough weed for five joints to be rolled. With this prison, Hardee C.I., being brand new and not at full capacity, there really isn't a market for weed yet. But that wouldn't last long. I am prepared to pinch off of my stash of weed every day until a window of opportunity opens to get in some more.

The next morning, after hearing the intercom sound off, "Work call! Work call! All inmates report to your assigned job locations. You have ten minutes to depart the dormitory."

I run my hand over the collar cuff of my military-style made bunk for the last time. I straighten up my shoes under Hollywood's bunk, reach into my locker, and grab my eye drop bottle and squeeze out three drops of Grey Flannel cologne and apply some to my neck, chest and arms. I lock my locker and leave the dormitory.

It is a beautiful, Sunshine State morning in Bowling Green, Florida. Too bad it had to be spent inside of this prison. I'd love to be anywhere else but here right now but I can't go back, I can only go forward. I have to pay my debt to society through blood, sweat, and tears, as is often quoted by the prosecutors within the Florida judicial system. What they didn't know is that all prisons aren't created equal. With that being said, this opportunity to work in the Medical Department feels like a breath of fresh air.

"Helimite. Whassup?" I look to my left and see Nardo in the canteen line.

"Whassup Nardo?"

Nardo responds, "I missed breakfast this morning. I'm buying a beef and cheese sandwich and a orange juice. You want something?"

"Yeah," I say, "Grab me two of those chocolate chip granola bars."

I stand off to the side of the line while Nardo orders the food. He leaves the window, hands me the granola bars and says, "I gotta get to work."

I say, "Yeah, me too."

Nardo asks, "Where did they assign you to?"

I respond, "Medical Department."

He looks at me with a smirk on his face and says, "Oh that's why you smelling like the Avon lady. Is that Brut 33?"

I laugh and say, "Hell naw, big homie. I'm not wearing no Brut 33. This is Grey Flannel!"

Nardo looks at me and says, "These rednecks gon' kill you up here 'bout them white women in that medical building."

I respond, "Nardo, I been dead ever since the judge gave me them fifty-five years. I'll rap with you later this evening." I head toward the Medical building officer's station.

I approach the fiberglass window. A female officer named Ms. Perch turns around in her chair and shouts, "What do you need, inmate?"

I say, "Good morning. I'm a Medical Orderly reporting to work, ma'am."

She hits the unlock button and the lock on the steel door releases. I step inside. Ms. Perch asks for my ID card and writes all the information on a log. She hands me my ID and hits another button for me to enter the main hallway into the medical department. It's 8 a.m. and the building smells like coffee and disinfectant.

A nurse comes out at one of the nurse's station, looks at me and asks, "Who are you here to see? We don't start seeing patients 'til 9 a.m."

I look her in the eyes and say, "Ma'am, I work here."

She calls out, "Rebecca! We don't have just one new orderly. We have two."

I could hear the sound of several chairs screeching across the floor as about six nurses, all white women, came into the hallway to look me over. I'm standing there with my starched-up prison blues on with my all white Travel Fox shoes, my GUESS watch, and my gold diamond cut rope chain against my brown skin, smelling so fresh and so clean.

I say, "Good morning ladies. My name is Helimite."

They all respond, "Good morning." And this one redhead named Rebecca steps toward me.

She was around 5'8" with a very petite shape and wore glasses. Next to her nametag were the letters R.N. embroidered into her V-neck medical scrubs.

Rebecca says, "Helimite, come with me, please."

I follow her down the hallway while doing my own look over at the same time. She was approximately 120 pounds and looked like she had on a pair of panties that were way too small because the panty line was so tight and right. She leads me to the doctor's office where Inmate Gene was already seated.

"Good morning, Dr. Smith," I say as I enter the room. I give Inmate Gene a handshake.

"Good morning, Inmate Helimite," Dr. Smith says, "Glad you could join us. As I was explaining to Inmate Gene, the first order of business for you young men is to report to the laundry this morning to pick up your work uniforms. Take this pass and hand it to the laundry Sergeant once you get there."

Inmate Gene and I leave Dr. Smith's office with some pep in our step. As we turn down one hallway and enter into the next, RN Rebecca asks, "Where are you two going?" as she pushes her glasses further up her nose with the other hand on her petite hip.

We respond, "To the laundry to pick up our work uniforms, ma'am."

She replies, "Well can you guys empty a few of these trash cans before you leave, please?"

"No problem, ma'am," I reply.

Inmate Gene and I go into six different offices and empty the trashcans. Every office I went into, the staff member occupying the room was courteous and curious all at the same time. My reason for saying that is because they all had questions when we entered their workspace. Will you guys be here all day? What prison are you guys coming from?

We were polite in our responses and kept it moving out the door. Once we left the medical building and was outside, I look at Inmate Gene and say, "Bro, what do you think?"

He looks at me and laughs then says, "Helimite, touch my forehead."

I touch his forehead and say, "You sick? Don't feel like   you   got   a   fever."

Inmate Gene responds, "I most definitely have a fever, Helimite, and it's Jungle Fever," referring to *Spike Lee*'s movie that explores interracial relationships.

I laugh and say, "Hell naw."

Inmate Gene goes on to say, "Before you arrived in the building, I was already inside looking the scene over. I only saw one black chick in the building and she works inside Medical Records and the way she looked, I seriously doubt she will interact with you and I at all."

I tell Inmate Gene, "You never know. She just might be the one."

We're walking and talking and heading in the direction of the laundry but we have to pass by the kitchen in order to get to the laundry. As we're passing the kitchen, someone speaks through the kitchen window, "Hey y'all brothers interested in some sausage, egg, and cheese sandwiches on toast?"

Inmate Gene and I stop dead in our tracks and say, "Hell yeah!" We walk toward the kitchen window where the voice was coming from.

"How many y'all want," the voice asks.

I say, "Give us two so I can see what you working with."

The voice inside the window pushed against the metal screen that wasn't completely bolted to the wall and slid two fat ass sandwiches out the window.

I asked the voice how much he wanted.

He said, "Two dollars."

I paid him and said, "Bro, what's your name?"

He says, "My name Hobo. I'm the head cook here from Orlando, Florida. Ivy Lane."

6

It's been a long week of nothing but adjustments. I had to adjust to my new work environment as well as all the new inmates that arrived at Hardee C.I. three times a week – Monday, Wednesday and Friday, courtesy of the Blue Bird prison bus. Inmate Gene was teaching me everything he knew pertaining to stripping, waxing and buffing floors. He mentioned to me that if I mastered this floor-cleaning process, I will never have a job in prison cutting grass, on a rake, or working the weed eater. You will always be inside in the air conditioning sniffing perfume and, if you play your cards right, sniffing panties as well.

I laugh and ask Inmate Gene, "Bro, you eat pussy?"

He responds, "I eat ass and pussy, Helimite. I have a ninety-five-year sentence and I have a parole hearing in ten years so any opportunity I get to explore a woman's body, I'm kissing and tasting every inch of her."

The look Inmate Gene had in his eyes as he spoke had me clearly convinced that he was dead ass serious. The floors in the medical building were looking like glass. The medical staff constantly asked us, "Are these floors still wet?"

"No, ma'am. We just put that wet look on it," we respond with a smile.

It's Friday and I am looking forward to hanging out tonight. I will smoke me a fat ass joint, watch reruns of *Miami Vice* until *Showtime at the Apollo* comes on, and at 12 midnight the Sooooooullllllllll Train! I already had my personal blue towel on the front row bench of the TV room to guarantee I could see and hear every word said on the show. We are allowed to stay up until two a.m. every Friday and Saturday night. Some inmates played poker, tonk, or shot dice until it was time to lock down.

The dorm that I was in had filled all the way up. There are a lot of new faces and a lot of bad attitudes. Nobody wanted to be at Hardee Correctional Institution mainly because it had nothing positive to offer yet. We are just being housed here to help eliminate a prison overcrowding problem. Keep in mind there is no chapel, no school, no vocational trades to be taught, no basketball courts, and last but not least, no mother fuckin' weed. Well, I had some weed but it wasn't for sale yet. It was for personal use only.

Every time someone smelled the weed I was smoking they would ask, "Bro, where is it at? You sellin' some? Who got it?"

I would respond, "I bought this from a Cuban dude yesterday," and keep it moving.

It may sound crazy to some but for everyone who is doing time and has done time, they understand the importance of weed being available to smoke while incarcerated. Weed knocks the edge off of everybody. It relaxes and calms all the tension and stress everyone is experiencing throughout a typical prison workday.

I'm sitting on the front row when I hear the *Soul Train* soundtrack come on. It's 12 midnight. The special guest tonight is *Tracy Spencer*. I guess she will be performing her hit song, *Tender Kisses*. The TV room is packed. I get up to get a drink of water and to get away from all the cigarette smoke. There are enough black people in this TV room to make a Spike Lee movie. There is not one white person in sight. I don't believe the judicial system is sentencing white people to prison yet. White people are getting sent to drug rehab, put on house arrest, or doing community service.

"Attention in the dormitory. Inmate Helimite report to the Officer's Station in Class A uniform, immediately."

It's 12:08 a.m. What the hell does the police want with me? There's a rumor out that the Florida Department of Corrections was going to start piss testing inmates for drug use soon. How soon, no one actually knew. I went to my room and got dressed. I wrote my mother's phone number on a piece of paper and handed it to my roommate Hollywood.

I told him, "I don't know what's going on but the police taking me somewhere. Call my momma if I don't return back to this room tonight."

Hollywood nods his head up and down and I leave the room. Once I get downstairs an inmate named Orange Man who is from Miami, shouts out, "Helimite, you gone?"

I say, "Yeah!"

He gets up off the back row of the TV room and sits on my towel in the front row. He looks back at the rest of the inmates in the TV room and says, "I just upgraded, negroes!" and the TV room erupts in laughter.

"Hey Helimite," Orange Man shouts out my name again.

I respond, "Yeah bruh, whassup?"

He shouts out, "Make them crackas kill you, dog! Make them kill you if they try some shit."

I throw up the black power sign, closed fist in the air, and walk out the dormitory door. I approach the Officer's Station and speak through the glass partition window.

"I'm Inmate Helimite, sir."

He responds, "Okay. Let me see your ID card."

I hand him my ID card through the sliding drawer beneath the partition window. He writes my information down on a log book then tells me to sit and wait. A few minutes later another officer enters the dormitory and tells me to turn around to be handcuffed.

I ask, "What for?"

He says, "All inmates must be handcuffed any time they are moving from one place to another at night."

I turn around and cuff up. I ask him, "Where am I being escorted to?"

He says, "You're a medical orderly, right?"

I respond, "Yes."

He states, "The Medical Department is being inspected on Monday morning by Tallahassee so you will be working the weekend at night to make sure all is in order."

I almost asked the Officer where Inmate Gene was but I chose to be *Still Quiet as Kept* and continued on to the Medical Building. Once I arrived the officer I was with, Officer Beers, opened the door with a key and removed my handcuffs. He went into the Medical Officer's Station Booth and hit the unlock button so I could enter the main Medical Hallway.

I will never forget what I smelt and what I heard when I entered that hallway. I could smell the perfume *White Diamonds* in the air and music was playing. The distinct hook of a Lisa Stansfield song echoed through the empty hallways.

Been around the world and I, I, I

I can't find my baby

I don't know when, I don't know why

Why he's gone away

And I don't know where he can be, my baby

But I'm gonna find him

And as if on cue, Nurse Bracey steps into sight.

7

"Shhhh!! Y'all be quiet," MullyGut says with one big black crooked finger placed to his lips. "Helimite, why did you bring them with you?"

I respond, "I didn't bring nobody. They followed me after I won all their marbles."

"Shhhh!! Just be quiet and watch," MullyGut says as he approaches the window once again.

The window is downstairs in the front of Stonybrook. It's dark outside and I can hear the Rick James song loud and clear.

She's a very freaky girl

The kind you don't take home to mother

"What y'all lookin' at? Let me see," Sam and Marvin says with a sense of urgency.

"Let me see!!"

There is a crease between the curtains that we can look through, with one eye, to watch this grown lady named Peaches touch her private parts. She is moving in slow seductive motions as her body glistens with sweat.

"One of these days I'm going to knock on her door and ask her to stop teasing me," MullyGut says.

I respond, "You think she know we watching, MullyGut?"

"Maybe, Helimite. I don't know," MullyGut says.

Peaches gets out of her bed and leaves the bedroom.

"The show is over. Let's keep it moving y'all," MullyGut says.

Growing up in Stonybrook, there was never a dull moment. There was always something to get into whether it was right or wrong and Friday nights we peeped in all the downstairs windows in the Stonybrook Apartment Complex.

"Oh shit. Y'all look who butt ass naked, dancing in her mirror," MullyGut whispers.

I rush to the window that MullyGut is standing at, with Sam and Marvin on my heels. I peep inside the window and ask, "Is that Bumble Bee?"

"Yes, it is," MullyGut says.

"Damn she got alotta hair around that coochie," Sam comments while standing on his tippy toes, trying to get a better view.

"Girls mature faster than boys. Ain't that right, Helimite."

"Shoot. I don't know. Why you say that, MullyGut?"

"I read it in Jet Magazine or Ebony somewhere," MullyGut replies.

"Let's keep moving y'all. I don't want her to see me peeping in her window and wanna fight me again. She beat me up one time before already."

"How you let a girl beat you up, Helimite?" MullyGut asks.

"She ain't no girl. She a tomboy."

"Thas still a girl, Helimite," Sam says.

"Man, y'all can say what y'all want. That tomboy undefeated in Stonybrook. I saw her fight my cousin Fly and everybody say it was a tie. Best fight I seen since we moved to Stonybrook."

"Let's go y'all," our fearless leader says and we continue on to another building.

We spread out and start looking in windows until somebody finds some action.

Marvin says in a hushed tone, "Y'all come here."

We head his way and Sam asks, "Wassup?"

He points to a window and says, "Y'all gotta see how big this man dick is."

MullyGut, Sam, and I look at Marvin real hard for a moment and MullyGut says, "We should beat yo' bitch ass up. We not peeping in windows to dick watch. We trying to see some coochie. Now take yo' bitch ass on your way. Talkin' about how big somebody dick is!"

MullyGut balled up his fist to punch Marvin in the face but Marvin wasn't having none of that. Marvin could have made the U.S. Olympic track team that night, he was moving so fast. Sam threw a rock at him but it didn't come close. We shook our heads and continued on with our tour. We finally hit the jackpot at K-Building. We caught two women in bed together licking on each other. I couldn't believe my eyes. I was only in the 5th grade and I knew that I would never forget this moment.

"What the hell they doing?" I ask MullyGut.

"The 69," MullyGut answers.

"What's the 69?" I ask.

MullyGut responds, "You looking at it, Helimite."

Sam is speechless and so am I.

"It's time to shake this freak show up a little bit," MullyGut says.

At this point he bangs on the window three times and takes off running. Sam and I take off in the opposite direction laughing so hard that our stomachs were cramping.

We go sit inside the Stonybrook Laundromat and start beating on the folding tables and freestyle rapping.

My name is Helimite

I have the heart of a lion

I never give up

I just keep on trying

Before I can spit another verse, I hear the squeaking sound of the entrance door to the laundromat opening. It's Niecy and her mother, Ms. Mary.

"Hey Ms. Mary, you need any help with your clothes' baskets," I ask.

"No, Helimite but I do need you to get yo ass outta hea, beating on these folding tables like y'all RUN DMC. I already have a headache."

"Yes, ma'am," I respond.

Niecy looks at Sam with a flirtatious smile and says, "Sam, your lil brother Derek is looking for you. I think your mama wants you."

Sam looks at me and says, "Helimite, I'll see you tomorrow."

I respond, "Ok, Archie Ball," Sam's rap name, "Bring me some of the pretty marbles you got tomorrow so I can beat you out of them."

Sam says, "Helimite you won all my marbles today. I'm broke."

I reach down in my pocket and pull out eight marbles and hand them to Sam and say, "You my best friend and if I can help you not be broke, I will. But don't play against me anymore, Sam. I shoot these marbles like a pro."

We laugh and give each other a hand slap and head home.

Stonybrook had some of the prettiest grass I had ever seen until we started to play football on it. The apartment manager Mr. Rudy was always running us off the grass, which left us nowhere to play but the parking lot. If your ass couldn't catch or play defense, you never got picked. We were so good as kids we took our teams to other neighborhoods to play whenever we could.

I run up the stairs to our apartment, F-202. I walk through the door and from out of nowhere I am blindsided with a slap. Bammm!!!

"Boy! Where you been?" my momma screams.

"You know you supposed to be in this house before the street lights come on. You thought I had left for church already."

I saw my mother's body twitch as she began to launch another slap to my head but my natural instincts took over and I ducked before it arrived. Man, why did I do that? My momma grabbed whatever was within reach to hit me with.

My stepdad said, "Dot we already late for church. I'll put him on punishment when we get back."

She looks at me and says, "I don't know what has gotten into you, son, but I rebuke it in the name of Jesus. Devil, my son is off limits. I rebuke you Satan and your assignment against him. I plead the blood of Jesus over him and declare that he will be used for the kingdom of God and His glory."

My mother continues, "Bring me that prayer oil off my dresser, Teresa."

My older sister comes out with the prayer oil. My momma calls me to her. As soon as I am close enough to her, she slaps me again and says, "Don't you ever duck when I swing. Now go wash up and eat."

8

"Well, good morning Inmate Helimite," Nurse Bracey says with a smile on her face.

"Good morning," I respond.

"You ready to work?" she asks.

"Yes, ma'am," I nod.

"Please don't start the ma'am thing. You make me feel old when you say that so let's make a deal. Only say it when other staff is around. We are the only ones here in the building tonight so relax, okay?" Nurse Bracey explains.

"Yes, ma'am. I mean, yes Nurse Bracey. Inmate Gene won't be coming to help out tonight?" I ask.

"No," she responds, "I only called for you. I'm pretty sure you can handle whatever needs to be done in this building tonight," she grins with a mischievous smile.

She is wearing an all-white nurse uniform and I can see the color of her underwear through the thin pant material. She instructs me to follow her and I comply. As she leads the way to the caustic closet, I'm watching her plump ass bounce from left to right until she finally comes to a stop. She reaches into her pocket and pulls out some chewing gum and a set of keys.

"Do you know which key opens this caustic closet, Inmate Helimite?"

"I sure don't," I respond.

She sighs and starts trying different keys. She finds the right key after several tries and props the door open with a door stopper. She turns to face me and asks, "You want a piece of gum?"

I respond, "I'll get one later."

She says, "Ok," and walks away.

I ask Nurse Bracey, "Why are your eyes so glossy?"

She laughs and says, "Because I'm high as a kite and I forgot my visine."

I respond, "Don't worry, Nurse Bracey, I'm *always quiet as kept* so your secret is safe with me. I actually wish I had a joint to burn myself."

"Well, Inmate Helimite, if I remember correctly you said you're an athlete and you don't do drugs."

"To be honest with you Nurse Bracey, I had just met you and felt like you were asking me a trick question. I smoke like a chimney whenever it's available."

She responds, "Aw hell. Me too! Only difference is it's available to me all the time."

"How is that?" I ask.

"My brother has a grow house in our barn. He grows the hydroponic weed that's also known as kryptonite. You ever heard of that?" She asks.

"Hell yeah, I heard of it but never sampled any before," I tell Nurse Bracey.

"Ok then. I'll give you half of the joint I brought with me today."

I'm standing there looking at this White girl who is clearly high as fuck saying to myself, 'please don't let this be a dream'.

"Nurse Bracey, how old were you when you started smoking weed?"

"I started in the ninth grade. I stayed under the bleachers at our school getting high so much they started calling me Bleacher Creature."

I responded, "Wow. That wasn't nice."

"Yeah but I didn't let it get to me back then. I was so into girls that nothing else really mattered. It was weed and girls or girls and weed."

"Well Nurse Bracey, you are most definitely talking my language."

She laughs and says, "You're so crazy Darrell... I mean Helimite."

"I guess Darrell holds a special place in your heart because even though you were into girls, Darrell is one person you can't seem to forget. I guess the old saying must be true..."

"And what's that Helimite?" Nurse Bracey asks.

"Once you go Black, you can't go back," I laugh.

She smiles and says, "I can only speak for myself and all I can say is 'hell yeah'."

"Well at least you're honest," I say as I walk into the closet and grab a broom, the buffer, a mop bucket and a gallon of wax along with several 'wet floor' signs.

I walk back toward the front of the Medical Building and push the button on the wall to get Officer Beers attention. He hits the unlock button and I walk into the Medical Lobby and begin to sweep while Officer Beers watches me like a hawk. I grab the dustpan and sweep all the dirt in it and flush it down the inmate bathroom toilet. I walk out of the bathroom and Officer Beers is standing up watching me now so I walk toward the officer's station partition window and say, "Officer Beers, it's okay. I've already been caught, tried, and convicted."

He looks at me and says, "Not on my watch, Inmate Helimite."

"What do you mean? Not on your watch?"

He responds, "Nothing out of the ordinary will happen during my eight-hour watch, if I can help it."

I nod my head up and down and say, "I can respect that."

I grab my mop and put way too much wax on the floor to keep his ass from walking on it. I place three 'wet floor' signs down and ask Officer Beers to open the door back into the main medical hallway. Nurse Bracey was jamming her Lisa Fischer CD.

How can I ease the pain

When I know you're coming back again

The song echoed through the empty hallways.

Nurse Bracey reappears and says, "Here you go," and hands me half a joint.

I slide it into my pocket and I explain to her that I'm about to put a coat of wax on this floor. "If you need anything from the offices in this hallway, you need to get it now."

She goes into one office and grabs a hand full of medical files and heads to the back of the Medical Department. I place two 'wet floor' signs on the floor and begin to apply a nice coat of wax that wouldn't dry for at least an hour. I waxed all the way into the next hallway where there was a door leading to the Dental Department. I was determined to deter Officer Beers from coming out of the Officer's Station booth. If he did, he was guaranteed to slip and bust his ass on the floor.

I turned the CD player off and take a look at the CD's in her collection. To my surprise, she had *Beastie Boys, Bobby Brown*, and several other R&B artists but what really shocked me was the *2 Live Crew* CD, *As Nasty as They Wanna Be*. Nurse Bracey had to be lights, camera, action and Helimite planned to be the main character in that porn movie. But business always before pleasure.

I walk into the Infirmary Nurse's Station and ask Nurse Bracey, "How much does an ounce of that kryptonite, that your brother grows, cost?"

She replies, "$200 an ounce."

I nod my head up and down and ask, "What will you charge me to bring two ounces?"

"Nothing," she said, "if you can provide the $400 to pay for the two ounces."

I'm looking at her and thinking to myself the combination of her being high and my resemblance to her ex-boyfriend Darrell has her wide open to whatever I'm putting on the table right now.

So, me being the hustler I am, I decide to seize the moment and say, "I'll pay you a thousand dollars for you to bring me four ounces. You bring them on whatever day you feel comfortable. I don't wanna know the date or time you plan to do it. I'll have the money already hid in this building so when the time comes, there's no delay in you receiving your cash."

She looks at me with those glossy eyes and says, "I'll do it under one condition."

I ask, "What?"

She says, "Tell me how in the hell do you have access to a thousand dollars in prison. Most people in society don't even have a thousand dollars in their bank account."

I respond, "I'm a hustler. I loan shark. I sell wine and I played a lot of poker at the last prison I was housed at."

She shakes her head in amazement and continues to stare right into my eyes. I break the silence, "Nurse Bracey…"

"Yes, Helimite," she answers.

"Can I have a piece of gum now, please?"

She reaches into her pocket to give me a piece of gum and I grab her arm and say, "Not the gum in your pocket. Give me the gum you're already chewing on."

She smiles and tries to reach into her mouth with her other hand.

I grab her hand and say, "Let me get it."

I press my lips against her as she pushes the gum and her tongue into my mouth with one swift motion. We kiss passionately for about three minutes while I grip her ass with my left hand and exploring her body with my right hand. I was inside her panties now playing with her clitoris as her breathing begins to intensify. I penetrated the wetness of her vagina and begin to finger fuck her with a slow and steady rhythm.

She kisses me harder and whispers, "Don't tease me, Helimite. Fuck me!"

My dick is hard as the concrete outside. I pull my fingers out of her wetness and use that same hand to move the hair away from her face. As I did that, the smell of fish was in the air. I asked Nurse Bracey, "What's that smell?"

She answers, "I don't smell anything. Fuck me, Helimite."

I bring my right hand to my nose and the smell of fish overwhelms me. As much as I desired to fuck my very first white girl, my brain had already sent a message to my dick to stand down. I was no longer hard and no longer interested in trying to fuck Nurse Bracey.

"But what about the weed, Helimite?" a voice in my head says.

I respond to the voice in my head, "Remember, we both got the same dick. I'm not fucking her! But yeah, you got a point, voice in my head!"

So, I guide Nurse Bracey back into her chair and pull out my extremely soft penis and say to her, "Get it hard for me."

She covered me with her lips as I grew inch by inch in her mouth. She took me out of her mouth as she began licking and sucking my balls. This feels so good that I am standing on my toes. She puts me back inside her mouth again and starts sucking on me like her life depends on it.

Then, all of a sudden, she stops and says, "Fuck me, Helimite. You will cum faster."

I look down at Nurse Bracey and respond, "Honey. I'm not interested in cumming fast. Just keep sucking."

She complies and ten minutes later I shoot a load of sperm into her mouth. She catches it then spits it out into a nearby towel. I pull up my pants and head down the hallway to the caustic closet to get some bleach to kill the scent of fish on my fingers. Who would have ever thought that a nurse's pussy wouldn't smell fresh. I thought hygiene and cleanliness was a mandatory standard for a nurse. The sad part about it is that I don't have the nerve or the nuts to even tell her. I figured that information would be humiliating to her and would cancel our agreement on the four ounces of weed.

Helimite, what have you gotten yourself into now? Before the voice in my head could answer, I hear the sound of a walkie-talkie and there was Officer Beers trying to creep in through the Dental Department door.

9

The next morning, I jump off my top bunk, take a piss, brush my teeth, wash my face and

thank God for allowing me to see another day. I slept right through breakfast so I reach into my locker and grab two packets of oatmeal, pour them into a bowl and add two spoon full of peanut butter. I go downstairs to add hot water and stir. I thought about calling my momma but I remembered it was Sunday and she would be in church, praising the Lord.

The P.A. system comes to life and the voice on the microphone says, "The yard is open."

I finish my bowl, put on some shorts and a V-neck shirt, grab my radio and head out the door. It's a partly cloudy morning, around 75 degrees Fahrenheit. I walk out to the softball field and head to the outfield, sit my radio down in the grass and start stretching then I hear someone call my name, "Helimite!"

I look up and to my surprise it's Ed "Jelly" Harper, the unofficial Mayor of Pleasant City in West Palm Beach, who had just arrived here on the Blue Bird prison bus last week.

"Wassup with you Jelly," I ask.

He responds, "I'm holding on by faith, Helimite. That's all I can do."

"I can dig it," I reply. "I'm about to workout, Jelly. Do you wanna ride with me?"

"Helimite, the only workout I'm doing is with a spoon in my hand," and he pats his stomach and laughs.

"You heard anything from the home turf lately?" I ask Jelly.

"Yeah, the Feds is cracking down on Palm Beach County. Banny Boy, Gangster Wimp, and all the Miami Boys that used to be on Third and Rosemary have all been swept up. So, a lot of new players are stepping into the drug game now completely in the blind on knowing all the specifics on what they are going to expose themselves and their families to." Jelly was choosing his words carefully and was in deep thought at the same time.

"Jelly, I gotta get this workout on before the sun decides to turn the heat up. We can get together third yard and catch up."

"Ok, Helimite. See you later."

I start doing body squats, fifty a set and fifty jumping jacks behind that. I'm pacing back and forth, catching my breath, when I notice to my left five guys with jackets on, fifty yards away. The smallest guy in the group appears to be the one in charge as he instructs the other four guys to position themselves in a certain stance. After the smaller guy was satisfied with their positioning, he stepped three feet away and began to give commands like a drill sergeant. The other four guys began to move in unison. It was poetry in motion. It was some kind of self-defense or karate class they were having. I laughed to myself and said, "Damn, karate classes in prison."

I continue with my workout and when I finished I went and bought an orange juice and a blueberry muffin. I walk to the bleachers and sit down with my radio next to me while jamming some song by a new female group that called themselves, *SWV*. The song was named, *I'm So Into You*. I fire up half the joint that Nurse Bracey had given me the night before and my lungs expanded on the very first pull of the joint. I was coughing hard. I was extremely high and I decided right then and there that I was in love with *SWV*. Their voices, anyway. They had to be singing about me especially as good as I was looking these days.

I had heard enough stories about guys buying females all kinds of gifts because of their fine bodies and pretty faces. Well, I had a fine body and handsome face the last time I looked so I intended to reverse the game whenever the opportunity presented itself.

"So Helimite, you plan on being a stripper when you get out," the voice in my head asked.

"Hell no. You know I can't dance at all," I respond to myself.

The karate people are still doing their thing. They're practicing kicks and throwing punches with them hot ass prison jackets on. If I wear a jacket in this kind of weather, you best believe I have a pipe that won't bend inside my sleeve and someone at the prison has a serious beat down coming their way. I grab my radio and head back to the dorm. I need to take a shower before they announce the twelve-noon count.

I enter the dorm and head upstairs to my room. I get to my room door and my roommate Hollywood has a homemade sign covering the window that says, "I'm taking a shit." So, I go back downstairs and sit down in the TV Room and watch and listen to the NFL commentators talk about how electrifying Prime Time Deion Sanders has been for the Atlanta Falcons. The 49ers need to find a way to get Deion Sanders on our team, I say to myself.

"Attention in the dormitory, all inmates report to your room for count and secure your doors."

I look upstairs. Hollywood has finally taken the sign down. I head back up the stairs and enter the room to the smell of baby powder and shit. Hollywood had made an attempt to kill the smell of shit by blowing baby powder all over the room. I climb up on my top bunk and sit there in an upright position waiting for security to come through and count. There's no exhaust system in a prison cell so the smell of shit and baby powder is still lingering.

I look down at my roommate and ask, "Hollywood, you don't flush as you go?"

Hollywood looks at me with a dumbfounded look as if to say, "What the hell you talking about, Helimite?"

So, I explain it to him in 'hood language. "As you're dropping a turd, flush the toilet at the same time. That way, the smell of shit doesn't get a chance to funk up the whole room."

Hollywood looked at me and replied, "Are you some kind of shit coach, Helimite?"

"Naw, Hollywood but we live in a small ass cell together so I'm sure you don't want to have to smell a load I may have to drop in the future especially with all the beans I eat."

He laughs and so do I.

Security comes and goes and count clears ten minutes later. Security unlocks the doors and I head straight for the shower. I walk into the shower stall and close the door. I turn the hot water on and immediately turn it back down. The water in the showers gets hot enough to make a cup of coffee. I lather up and start to think about how Nurse Bracey gave me head the night before. But the more I thought about how stink her vagina was, I slowly lost my erection and couldn't get it back up to masturbate in this shower. More kids have died in these prison showers than any abortion clinic in America. I dry off and head back to my room with just a pair of gym shorts and a towel in my hand.

The intercom in our dorm comes to life, "Inmate Helimite, you need to have a shirt on going to and from the shower room."

I nod in agreement and enter into my room. I begin to get dressed in my all white medical orderly uniform when

I hear the intercom announce that it's chow time. I look out the window to make sure Hollywood is leaving the dorm to go eat. As soon as he does, I grab my homemade screwdriver and go into my radio and count out a thousand dollars cash. I put five hundred in each shoe and try to head out the door but it's already locked. I mash the officer station button for service.

The officer says, "What's up?"

I say, "Can you let me out, please?"

"No. You missed your opportunity to go eat already," the officer explains.

"Sir. I'm not going to eat. I'm going to work. Tallahassee is doing a big inspection Monday in the Medical Department so I'm waxing and buffing all the floors, sir."

The officer pops the door with no further conversation. Whenever you tell a Correction Officer, "Tallahassee is coming for an inspection," they all get nervous feeling as though their jobs might be in jeopardy.

I head toward the Medical Department. I show the Officer that's there today my ID card. He logs it in on a clipboard and pushes the button for me to enter. Once I enter the main hallway I empty the trash cans from every office. I make a right at the end of the hallway where the break room is located on my left. I hear two females conversing inside the break room.

I enter and speak. "Good afternoon, ladies."

They look up from their meal completely startled.

"Inmate Helimite, I didn't know you were in the building."

"I just arrived, Nurse Everette, to do a walk through to make sure all is in order."

She responds, "You need to wear latex gloves whenever you're cleaning, Inmate Helimite."

"I'll go grab a pair right now," I tell her.

"Hold on a minute," Nurse Everette says, "Have you met Nurse Precious?"

"No I haven't," I say as I turn my head to focus my attention on Nurse Precious. I had to catch my breath. Nurse Precious had long flowing black hair. Her skin looked as if it was kissed by the summer sun, bronze and shiny. She looked like she was from a foreign island in the Caribbean.

"Nice to meet you, Nurse Precious."

I quickly regroup and say, "I need to finish making my rounds so I can watch some NFL football today, ladies. Enjoy your lunch."

"Thank you," they both say.

As I'm leaving the break room I hear Nurse Everette say, "So Precious, tell me all about your 27th birthday party over in Brazil and don't leave anything out."

I'm heading back down the hallway to get a pair of latex gloves. A box full of gloves is sitting on the counter in the Nurse's Station next to a box of alcohol pads. I grab about fifty alcohol pads, stuff them in my back pocket, put on my latex gloves, and continue to make my rounds.

Nurse Precious was beyond good-looking. In my eyes, she is gorgeous. I could tell she was fine just by looking at her hips and how fat her thighs were, sitting down. I head to the Infirmary Nurse's Station and grab a roll of medical tape off of the counter. I take off one of my shoes and remove five one-hundred dollar bills from its hiding place between my foot and the sole of my shoe. I tape the cash behind a filing cabinet and then circle the hallway again to make sure the nurses were still eating in the break room.

They were just leaving the break room as I bent the corner. Just as I had predicted, Nurse Precious, 27 (my new nickname for her), was walking toward me with a box of *Krispy Kreme* donuts in her hand. She was wearing a pair of green nurse pants so tight, all you could see was a gap between her legs. My whole insides are burning with lust and I was growing an erection as I stood there.

"Inmate Helimite…"

"Yes," I respond.

"Would you like a donut?" Nurse Precious asks.

"Yes ma'am. Sure. I love *Krispy Kreme* donuts," as I reach for two.

"I'm up here. Not down there," Nurse Precious says and looks me dead in my eyes.

I sigh. I can't believe I let her catch me looking at that fat cat. Hell, she knew what she was doing when she got dressed this morning and looked into that full-length mirror and jacked them pants up into her crotch area.

I put my two donuts on a paper plate and place it inside the microwave for seven seconds. I remove it from the microwave and open the refrigerator. There are a few cartons of milk in there so I take one not caring who it belonged to. I sit down at the break table and eat my donuts and wash it down with the milk. My eyes are roaming over the break area for another good spot to hide some money. The best spot available was under the refrigerator. I check the hallway again, looking left to right, then take off my other shoe removing five more one-hundred dollar bills and tape it under the front side of the refrigerator.

I wipe down the break table and the counter where the microwave sits then head back down the hallway that leads to the medical lobby. I put on another pair of latex gloves, grab all the trash bags that I removed from the cans and head to the front door. I push the officer station button, hold up all the bags of trash for the officer to see. He unlocks the door and I proceed through the lobby. He unlocks the front door that leads to the compound and I carry the trash bags at least 20 yards away to the main trash dumpster behind the kitchen.

I take a deep breath and sigh. All my money is in place. If Nurse Bracey brings anything tonight I'll hide it until morning, add it to a trash bag and move it out of the building and eventually to the dorm.

"Sounds like a plan, Helimite."

"Shut up," I tell the voice in my head.

10

Sunday night lockdown is always 10 p.m. because Monday is a work day. Time seems to be flying by. Days turn into weeks. Weeks turn into months and months turn into years. Time seems to be moving right along. I put on my headphones, adjust my antenna and let my body relax as the song by Troop, *All I Do Is Think of You* plays. I'm wondering what Ms. Washington, a.k.a The Real One is up to now. Had she moved on to the next brother back at Polk and was Coach Willis still the Queen Bee? Damn, I miss Polk C.I.

"Helimite, you sound crazy! How can you lie here and say you miss damn prison," the voice in my head says.

"Let's be clear. You miss Coach Willis and Ms. Washington not the prison. Once you start saying stuff like that or feeling like that you have taken the first step into becoming institutionalized."

"Okay, voice in my head, you're absolutely right!"

I need to remember to call momma tomorrow, I'm thinking, as the D.J. at the radio station plays *Shirley Murdock I Still Love You.*

Fergie wrote me a letter telling me she dedicated that song to me the other night on Soul 16 WPOM out of West Palm Beach but I really feel like I'm on the other side of the world being in this prison. If God continues to wake me up every morning, I will make it back home one day! Let's see if all this love my ex-girlfriend is declaring can stand the test of time.

We were 14 years old when Fergie and I met in the parking lot at the Pizza Hut on 45th Street in Mangonia Park. At first sight, I understood why people always used to say "Black is Beautiful" because Fergie was jet black and so beautiful! When I asked her for her seven digits I had a pen but I didn't have anything to write on. I removed a ten-dollar bill from my pocket and wrote my phone number on it and gave it to her. She laughed and took the bill then called me later on that evening. We went out just a couple of times because her parents were very strict, God-fearing, Hilltop Church people and I was not exactly the type of guy they wanted their daughter dating. I will say this though; Fergie and her mother were in attendance at my trial every day.

*Luther Van*dross is singing *Wait for Love* but *Tina Turner* brings me back to reality with *What's Love Got to Do with It? Who needs a heart when a heart can be broken?*

I suddenly feel a hand on my feet, shaking them. As I prepare to kick my roommate in the face I hear a walkie talkie sound off and I open my eyes to see Officer Beers standing there.

"Inmate Helimite! Get Class A dressed for work. I'll wait for you downstairs."

I look at my watch and its 12:20 a.m. I get up and brush my teeth and wash my face and start to get dressed. I close my cell door behind me and head downstairs where Officer Beers is waiting with handcuffs. He tells me to turn around to be pat searched first.

I look at him and say, "It's too early in the morning for you to be rubbin' and feelin' on me, Officer Beers."

He gives me a surprised look and shouts, "That's a direct order!"

I comply with the order and allow him to handcuff me. I need to stay focused on the plan and not provoke this young ass rookie. I may need his help somewhere in the future but then again, he may need my help somewhere in the future.

Every neighboring prison of Hardee, which are Charlotte, Desoto, Lake, and Polk Correctional Institutions were all transferring their worst and most difficult inmates to Hardee C.I. to fill up all these empty bunks. Hearing this, I knew Hardee was going to be like a volcano ready to erupt with all kinds of violence. All these inexperienced officers weren't going to be ready for the wave when it came. The only thing keeping me away from it all was my working in the Medical Building throughout the majority of the day and now nights as well.

I take the short trip across the empty compound to Medical and say nothing. As Officer Beers removes my handcuffs I enter into the main hallway of Medical. I can smell food. I'm not sure what kind of food. I just hope Nurse Bracey did not try to offer me any because I would clearly need to decline. No way I was going to eat anything she cooked. The way her vagina smelled when I was intimate with her told me everything I needed to know about her hygiene habits.

I walk down the hall and stop where the smell of food was present. Nurse Bracey is sitting in the nurse's station eating and counting needles at the same time.

"Well hello Helimite," Nurse Bracey says as she turns to face me.

She smiles as she looks me over with her glossy eyes that seem to be twinkling at me.

"Good morning Miss Bracey. I guess you have the munchies from the look in your eyes and the brownies on your plate."

She laughs, stands up and gives me a hug.

"Can you help me count these needles? The day shift apparently can't find the time to do it, which leaves me to do inventory on our supplies."

I stand to the left side of her and begin to help count needles. As soon as we are done she asks me to follow her to the back to our caustic supply closet. Once inside, she reaches down inside her panties and pulls out what looks like a maxi pad but was really my first ounce of kryptonite weed. I grab it and tell Nurse Bracey that I'd be right back.

I go to my cash stash and get her 200 and place the ounce under the refrigerator. I return to where Nurse Bracey is and hand her the money.

She looks at me and says, "Be careful, Helimite. Please."

I nod my head up and down and say, "I'm **still quiet as kept** through thick and thin, my friend."

We hug and I tell her that I need to get to work so that Officer Beers doesn't get suspicious. I clean the Medical lobby and restroom as Officer Beers watches. Before I get done he waves for me to come toward the officer's station door. He opens the door and asks for me to empty his trash and to sweep and mop inside his work station as well.

"Inmate Helimite, how do you guys get steroids in here?"

I look at Officer Beers and say, "What are you talking about?"

"You guys have to be taking steroids. There are no weights at Hardee C.I. but you guys stay swol' up," Officer Beers replies.

I answer, "I do close to 600 pushups a day along with dips and pull-ups plus three-square meals a day and proper rest. No steroids in my system, just determination! I can write you up a workout plan if you're interested in buffing up."

He nods his head in agreement.

"I'll bring you one tomorrow. I'm ready to return to my dorm once I put all this cleaning material back up."

He responds, "Okay."

11

The next day came and went like a blur. Two busloads of inmates arrived. One from Charlotte C.I. and the other from Martin C.I. also known as the New Rock. I had been so busy assisting with the intake process I never had the opportunity to retrieve my ounce of kryptonite after working last night. My young body was starting to shut down. Sleep was very much needed so I went back to my dormitory to lay down. I tried to sleep but the noise they were making down at the domino table was unbelievable. The tables in the day room slash TV room were all steel bolted down to the concrete floor. These brothers were slamming the dominoes down, one by one, with a bang.

I grab the extra wool blanket I had at the end of my bed and take it down stairs to the domino table. When the game that was in session ends I say, "Fellas, if y'all don't mind, can you lay this blanket over the table to kill all the bang, bang, bang?"

The four brothers looked at me and a fella named 36, who I knew, took the blanket and spread it over the table then began to shuffle the dominoes. As I turn to walk away, a short stocky brother named Killer Miller says, "Who the hell that negro think he is? If he can't handle the noise, he need to bond out! This ain't the library!"

I look him over and say nothing, mainly because I'm not looking for any trouble. I notice the phone is wide open so I walk in that direction and take the phone off the hook. The phone was bolted to the wall but had a cord about three feet long. As I begin to dial my momma's number, Killer Miller walks up to me and states that he was next on the phone. I act like I can't hear him and keep dialing. What happened next, I can remember as clear as yesterday.

Killer Miller holds down the phone lever to cancel the number I was dialing and says, "I just told you I was next on this phone, playboy!"

I keep my composure and in my humblest voice I can muster I say, "I apologize. I didn't hear you brother."

As I begin to hand him the phone receiver, he had his face all balled up like he was in gorilla mode. I decide now would be the best time to tame this wanna-be-gorilla. I strike Killer Miller in the face across his left eye with the phone receiver and then slap him in the mouth with it as blood shot out like a fountain. He tried to back away from the beat down but I grabbed the inside of his V-neck prison shirt and kept bashing him. The three feet of phone cord gave me all the swinging mobility I needed to punish this wanna-be-bully.

All eyes were on me putting a whooping on dude when the dorm intercom sounds off, "All inmates lockdown! Immediately. That is a direct order. Lock it down now!"

The inmates in the dorm completely ignore the direct order. They weren't about to miss the very first fight at Hardee C.I. Blood was in the air and as long as my blood wasn't the blood being spilled I was grateful. I wasn't looking for any trouble but I wasn't running from it either. I placed the bloody phone receiver back on the hook, kicked Killer Miller in the stomach one good time as he lay on the ground then ran upstairs to my room. I grabbed all my property that was out, threw it in my locker and locked it. I changed my shirt and put the bloody shirt in my dirty clothes laundry bag.

Minutes later at least 20 officers rushed into the main dorm. A few officers were assisting Killer Miller on the ground and another officer was on his walkie talkie calling for medical attention. The other officers had everyone lock themselves in their rooms and then proceeded to visit every room, asking every inmate to take off their shirt and to show their hands to see if there were any visible injuries to identify the other inmate that was fighting.

When they get to my room I am cool, calm, and collected. I do everything they ask me to do saying, "Yes sir. No sir." The officer in the booth who made the original call that a fight was in progress was a rookie and didn't keep his eyes on the fight to identify all involved. Now y'all know the old saying with white people that all black people look alike. On this day I needed that to be true because I didn't want to go to confinement for 30 days right now. I had a real good thing going on in Medical and I didn't want to lose my position.

"You should've thought about that before you smashed the brother in the face with the phone receiver, Helimite," the voice in my head says loud and clear.

"Shut up! Nobody asked you anything. Whose side you on anyway?" I answer out loud.

My roommate Hollywood asks, "What you talking 'bout, Helimite?"

"Nothing, Hollywood. I'm just thinking out loud."

I look out my front door and notice Captain Wiley has entered the dorm and has all the officers huddled up, giving them instructions. I wish I could hear it. The officers disperse and begin to enter each cell again. Once they get back to my cell they search it and paid close attention to the clothing items. They found my dirty laundry bag, dumped it out and bingo – they found my bloody prison shirt with my name on it. They cuff me up and escort me to the captain's office. Once I get there, Captain Wiley asks me about the incident. "Why were you fighting with Inmate Miller?"

I stood there and said nothing.

"Oh. You one of them convicts that don't do no talking."

After three or four more attempts to get me to talk I finally say, "No matter how many times you ask me the same questions, several different ways, several different times. Sir, I'm **still quiet as kept**."

I pause and take a deep breath, contemplating what's ahead of me. "Captain Wiley, I'm tired. These handcuffs and shackles are too tight and cutting against my skin. Can you please have your staff take me to my new cell in confinement?"

He shook his head in disgust and told the officers that are escorting me to loosen my cuffs and shackles. "Take him to Medical for a pre-confinement check then take him to confinement," Captain Wiley instructs the staff.

12

When I finally make it to confinement I am so tired. Between the fight and the interrogation process, I fall asleep as soon as I enter my new one-man cell. I wasn't even asleep for an hour yet when the confinement officers bang on my door. "Hey Inmate Helimite! What's the combination number to your locker so we can inventory your property and bring you all the approved property you can have while in confinement."

"22 left, 31 right, 15 left," I tell them and fall right back to sleep. When I wake again it's breakfast time in confinement. 5 a.m. Grits, eggs, two biscuits, grape jelly, milk and an orange. I ask the inmate serving the trays if he had any extra trays for sale. He answers that he does have extra and I ask him how much.

"Five stamps," he answers.

Postage stamps is your only source of trade while in confinement. It is currency.

I tell him, "I don't have my property yet but I'll give you the stamps bro. My word is all I got."

He asks, "What's your name?"

"Helimite," I answer.

"Don't worry about the stamps. Hobo the head cook told me to look out for you."

I nod my head up and down and say, "Bet that up and tell Hobo I appreciate that. What's your name brother?"

He answers, "Norm Skee."

"Where you from?"

"St. Pete!"

"Okay. Can you tell them officers I need my property and a phone call to cancel my visit that's coming this weekend?"

Norm Skee answers, "I'll let them know."

I ask, "Norm Skee. How you get that nickname?"

"That's my rapper name!"

I glance at Norm Skee, "Oh so you can flow."

Norm Skee responds with the quickness, "I'm the best on the compound. If they have a talent show during Black History Month here, I will bless the mic."

Norm Skee was about 5'6" and had a bounce to his walk. He had to be around the same age as I was. He had no hair on his face at all. We were still too young to grow any. I had just started seeing a little mustache myself. It's shocking at the amount of young, Black men being sent to prison at such a young age.

The intercom came to life and an announcement was made for sick call. "The nurse is making her rounds. If you're sick, stand at your door in your Class A uniform."

It's 6:30 a.m. now and I hear the front door to the cell block open and to my surprise it's an officer escorting Nurse Bracey from cell to cell. When she gets to my cell I say that I need some Tylenol and some jock itch powder. She looks at me and asks, "What are you doing back here?"

"Supposedly a fight, ma'am."

"What do you mean supposedly? You either was fighting or not," Nurse Bracey responds.

The officer with Nurse Bracey steps up and says, "You know this inmate, Nurse Bracey?"

She says, "Yes. He's one of our Medical Orderlies. Open his food slot."

The officer opens the slot. She hands me the Tylenol, winks at me and says, "I'll bring the jock itch powder tomorrow," and walks away.

I lie on my bunk. I hear footsteps at my door. It is two officers with a pillow case filled up with my property that I can have in confinement. They tell me to turn around and cuff up. I comply. They open my cell door and set my property inside my cell then shut the door. I stick my hands back through the food slot and they uncuff me. The first thing I grab is my radio. Since I hadn't received a disciplinary report yet or been found guilty of any rule violation, they had to give me all my property except for sharp objects like shaving razors or tweezers.

I tune my radio immediately to the AM station 1380. This station is as close as I was going to get to the AM station SOUL 16 or FOXY 1040 that I listen to back home. I place all my property in my locker and listen to *R. Kelly* and *Public Announcement* sing about *Honey Love*. As I lie there replaying what lead up to the fight, I have no regrets. If I wouldn't have stopped Killer Miller in his tracks, it would have only gotten worse so it's whatever.

I get up, grab my photo album, and start looking at all the beautiful young sisters I grew up with. I stop on a page with some pictures of Beth, her cousin Rhonda, and Shorty Brown hanging out at the annual Art Festival at Gaines Park. I prop the album up against the wall like an open book and begin to do pushups on my knuckles and body squats. 25 per set. I was wishing I was with Beth, Rhonda, and Shorty Brown at Gaines Park looking at the exotic African art, listening to the music, and sampling all the different food.

Confinement is a mental thing. Some can handle it and a lot of inmates can't. The walls feel like they are closing in after a while. There's nobody to talk to and you're hungry all the time unless you came to confinement with food already in your property or can afford to buy extra trays from the confinement orderly. Me, on the other hand, I'm never lonely. I pray and talk to God. I listen to my radio and look through my photo album. Those pictures are worth a thousand words.

After seven working days had passed I ask the Confinement Sergeant what day I was scheduled to go to DR court. He tells me that I don't have a disciplinary report and that I'm just under investigation.

"For how long?" I ask.

He responds, "They can hold you back here for six months if they want."

"Six months?" I repeat! "Listen Sergeant, my mother is coming to visit me this weekend. I need my one phone call to cancel that visit before she drives five hours for nothing.

Sgt. Morales looks at me and says, "Sit tight. I'll have one of my officers come get you to use the phone."

I say, "Thank you sir!"

Thirty minutes later Officer Larison, who I nicknamed Vanilla Ice, comes and puts me in handcuffs, opens my door, and escorts me to the phone. I dial my momma's number.

"Praise the Lord, my son." My momma's voice comes through loud and clear. "I haven't heard from you in a while. You okay?"

"Yes momma, I'm okay. I'm calling to tell you I'm in confinement right now and can't receive any visits while I'm in confinement."

"What happened, son?" she asks.

"I got into a fight," I reply.

My momma quickly responds, "Son, you've been fighting your whole life. When are you gonna stop and just give them problems to God?"

"Momma, I have never fought anyone because I wanted to fight. It's because I had to. Look at all them fights and wars that took place in the bible. The bible say it's a time for war and peace."

"So, son is that all you learned in Sunday School all them years? Are you injured?"

"No ma'am. I handled it Ma," I respond.

"Is that your way of saying you won?"

"Yes."

"Well, my son, nobody wins when you fight because someone got hurt."

"Momma, I'd rather it be them that got hurt and not your favorite son!"

"I never said you was my favorite. I love all my children the same."

"You always told me, momma, you gotta claim it to receive it so I claim that I'm your favorite son in Jesus' name!"

The laugh my momma let out filled my soul with her spirit. "I gotta go momma. I'll call you when I get released from back here. I love you, 'Ma. Tell Teresa, Tan, Tamia, and Keyna I love them as well."

"Read the Book of Job while you're back there, son."

"Okay, 'Ma. Bye!"

I was in confinement for 21 days before the Prison Inspector came to interview me. The whole time that I had been in confinement I did not see Killer Miller. Not once. I found out he was being held in a medical isolation cell due to his injuries.

Inspector Patterson is a White female with dark blonde hair that she keeps in a bun at the base of her head. She smokes cigarettes every opportunity she can get. In fact, she was smoking a cigarette when she entered in to the Disciplinary Hearing room. The room is the size of a two-car garage. The air conditioning is blowing so cold in this room that I have chill bumps. The shiny new table I'm seated at is the only thing that separates me from the inspector.

She sits down, takes a drag of her cigarette and begins her line of questioning with, "What was the fight about?"

I respond, "I have no idea."

She leans forward, looks at me and says, "My time is valuable so please don't bullshit me, Inmate Helimite. So, you're telling me that you don't know why you were fighting Inmate Miller?"

I stretch my legs out under the table and I lean back in my chair before I answer her, "I wasn't fighting Inmate Miller, ma'am."

Inspector Patterson is wearing a well-fitted black pant suit with a gold inspector badge around her neck that hits the table as she asks me, "Well explain all the blood that was on your shirt."

I take a deep breath and sigh and explain to Inspector Patterson that I got the blood on my shirt from doing my job.

"What in the hell are you talking about, Inmate Helimite?" as she rises to her feet with a dumbfounded look on her face.

"Inspector Patterson, you're an inspector and it is your job to inspect. My prison file will reflect my job assignment here at Hardee C.I. is Medical Orderly! I have watched films on C.P.R. and how to deal with cuts and blood spills. I was assisting Inmate Miller to the best of my ability as he appeared to be bleeding to death and during that process his blood stained my clothing."

Inspector Patterson looked at me for a minute and pulled out another cigarette and lit it.

I continued, "The officers that worked that night checked my hands for scratches, cuts, and bruises. I had none because I wasn't fighting."

I already knew that they didn't have any evidence to identify me as the other person involved in the fight. Hardee C.I. was proving itself early to be **quiet as kept** and gangster in all its moves. Killer Miller wasn't saying anything because he wanted some revenge.

Inspector Patterson asks me to stay seated and she leaves the room. When she returns she states, "So you never saw who the other inmate was who assaulted Inmate Miller?"

"No, I didn't, ma'am."

"Ok then, I'll have you escorted back to your cell. I'll let you know something after my investigation is complete, Inmate Helimite."

I nod my head in agreement as she leaves the room firing up another cigarette.

I am escorted back to my one-man cell. I look out my back window and notice a few guys picking up trash behind my dorm. One of the inmates was my homeboy Nardo. I yell out my window, "Federal Gardens!"

He looks up and laughs. "Stonybrook, where you at?"

"Upstairs, third window, man."

"When they gonna cut you loose from back there?"

"I don't know. I don't have a D.R. I'm just under investigation. I just had a interview with the inspector. She says she will get back with me later. Wassup with Dr. Rock?"

"He up there working right now in Staff Canteen. You need anything?"

"Yeah, I do. I need a couple of boxes of those chocolate chip granola bars, some peanuts and two books of rolling paper."

"What you need rolling paper for, Helimite?

"If I tell you that, Nardo, I'll have to kill you so I'm gonna remain **quiet as kept** on that.

Nardo bust out laughing. "I got you Stonybrook."

"Ok Federal Gardens."

This is the part of confinement that gets to you, not knowing when you're going to be released from the box. But I have created a daily routine that passes the day away for me so I'm not losing my mind or hearing voices, banging on the door screaming to talk to the psychologist before I kill myself. Quite a few inmates have done just that. The box is just too much pressure for some.

13

It's been three days since I spoke with Inspector Patterson and still no word so I go inside my radio and pull out enough weed for two days. I roll the ugliest joint you ever seen but as long as it burns I'll be as high as an astronaut in this confinement cell. I stand on top of the steel toilet seat to put my face right next to the exhaust system to remove the weed smoke directly out of my cell and into the outside atmosphere.

I fire up and begin to smoke. As I blow the smoke in the vent, another inmate in a cell downstairs somewhere screams out, "I smell it. I smell it. Don't hide it. Divide it. Smoke with me like you joke with me."

He's making so much noise I put my joint out because, with all that noise, I know the police is going to make his rounds. I grab my Irish Spring soap and lather up a rag and wipe down the walls and the window where the fresh air enters the room. Ten minutes later the door to the cell block opens. Somebody screams, "Fire in the hole," meaning the police are in the building. The officer is making his rounds looking into every cell window.

He gets to my door and bangs on my door. Of course I'm playing like I'm asleep. "Inmate Helimite!"

"Yeah, whassup?"

"It's 'Yes sir.' You're not on the streets."

"Yes, sir."

"Pack your shit."

"For what?" I ask.

"You're being released to population. I'll be back to get you in thirty minutes," the officer says and keeps it moving.

The joy I felt at that moment was tremendous. It felt like I was being released to West Palm Beach, Florida instead of open population inside of a prison. The amount of freedom that is afforded to you in open population will have you flexing like you're in the free world. As I sit on my bunk waiting for that confinement door to open, all kinds of thoughts are going through my head. Will I be able to get my job back in Medical? What dorm will they assign me to now?

Twenty minutes later my door slides open. I step out and all the other inmates that weren't getting out start hollering and banging on their doors at me with all kinds of requests. Can you get that Essence magazine for me from Cell 10? Do you have any food you can leave a brother? And the most common request is, can you spare any stamps or envelopes? Me being the person I am left all I could for the brothers and passed around books and magazines to different cells until the P.A. system sounded off.

"If you don't bring your ass off that cell block right now, Inmate Helimite we gonna rebook your ass," the sergeant stated.

I leave with the quickness. I approach the Officer Station booth and was given a piece of paper with my new dorm and bunk number. It read Dorm 2A, Room #208. The confinement sergeant hit the unlock button for me to depart and as soon as I stepped outside on the sidewalk it began to thunder and a bolt of lightning came from out of nowhere. It came so close to me that all the hair on my body stood up and all I could do, from that point, was repent.

Father, in the name of Jesus, I repent of all my sins Lord. I ask that you spare my life as I walk these one hundred yards to this dorm. I grab my property and start stepping toward Dorm 2A. As the rain poured down on me, it felt good against my skin after being in confinement all that time.

"Attention on the compound! The yard is closed. All inmates report to your dormitory immediately."

Why security felt the need to say that, I don't know, because all the Black people I know are scared of thunder and lightning. I remember my momma always saying while I was growing up, "Y'all children sit down somewhere while God does his work. Don't get in the shower. Turn that T.V. and them lights off and Tanya – hang up that phone!" I used to be so scared that I'd get under my bed. I miss my momma and sisters.

I finally arrive at Dorm 2A. I enter the dorm and approach the officer station. A female sergeant named Rawls asks for my I.D. card, wrote down my information on a log book and pointed to the dorm I was now being housed in. The inmates inside the dorm were already looking through the glass windows at me. Some were curious about who I was. Others looking for signs of wealth – jewelry, expensive tennis shoes, and lots of canteen items were clear signs that you weren't broke.

As Sergeant Rawls hits the release button for me to enter 2A, I step inside and make a left turn to head up the all-blue steel flight of stairs. The dorm went silent for a good three minutes while everyone in there tried to figure out what room I was going to. I enter Room 208 and place all my property in my locker and begin to make up my bed. I grab my baby powder and shake a good amount across my mattress. I put a sheet over it. My pillowcase is soaked so I turn on the heater and lay my pillowcase across it to dry. I take my radio out and tune in to a jazz station.

I have no idea who my roommate is because he isn't present when I enter the cell. The officer announces, "15 minutes 'til 8:00 count." My door opens and this lil short brother, about 5'5", 175 pounds with a toothpick in his mouth, enters the room. He looks up at me and nods his head and I nod back as a form of speaking without speaking.

He locks the door and says, "I think your pillowcase is dry."

I hop down off the top bunk and check it. It's completely dry. I turn off the heater and get back on my bunk. I know I have seen this lil short brother somewhere before but I can't recall where. I fall asleep and wake for the 10:00 p.m. count and fall right back to sleep after giving my name and prison number to the officer. They count us at least eight times a day to make sure no one has escaped.

The thunder, lightning, and rain would have been the right moment for some fool to try to climb over that razor wire fence to reach free society only to be met with a bunch of lead from those AR-15 assault rifles the gun towers are equipped with.

I wake up to the sound of my door being opened at 4 a.m. "Inmate Bell, wake up. Get ready for work!"

My roommate works in the kitchen. That's always a good thing. There's no telling when I might need an onion, some garlic, honey, etc. Even if he is not hustling stuff out of the kitchen, I'm pretty sure he knows who is. I stretch my arm out, reach toward the window where my radio is and press the on button. *Earth Wind and Fire* is singing about *Reasons.* My roommate washes up and locks the door behind him.

I get off my bunk and search through my legal mail for all the Black Porn magazines I paid ten natural dollars for while at Polk C.I. I grab my baby oil grease up and start to flip through the pages at the same time. It doesn't take long before I'm as hard as the concrete I'm standing on. I'm using the night light from outside my door to see. I'm looking at some sister named Cinnamon and she is bent over looking at me, asking me to stand up in that pussy.

I'm jacking away like my life depended on it when I hear the front door down stairs open. It's a White female officer with a flash light doing the hourly head count. She comes straight up the stairs to start counting. I put the book and baby oil away and stand over the toilet like I'm pissing. I know the rules better than anyone. As long as I'm not stroking it with a back and forth motion she can't scream and write me up. This is a male prison so she is going to see some dick eventually and tonight is the night as *Betty Wright* used to sing about.

Now in some people's minds I'm being a pervert right now. In my defense, if I masturbate in front of her then I am a pervert but it's not going to happen. I'm going to stand at the toilet, pretending to be half asleep, rock hard, supposedly trying to urinate at 5:00 a.m. When her flashlight shines through my front door window she is startled at first but tries to remain professional. She shines the light on my greased up manhood for about ten seconds then walks away to continue counting. About three minutes later she does a recount and stops at my door, shining that flash light again.

I'm on my bunk now just lying there. She knocks on the door and says, "You okay in there?"

I hop off my bunk and approach the door and respond, "Yes. I'm okay. Why do you ask?"

She responds, "You appeared to be excited earlier when I came through on that first count."

"No, ma'am. Nothing to be excited about. Just trying to take a piss."

She responds, "You were gonna piss all over the wall and floor. The toilet is down and you were at full attention."

"Ma'am, I'm not gonna lie to you because I don't wanna get wrote up for lying to staff. When you looked in here the first time, I wasn't fully erect. That was what we call semi-hard or even soft."

She burst out laughing and said, "Whatever. You Black guys swear you have the biggest ding dongs on the planet."

She walks away chuckling and continues her rounds. Her name was Ms. O'Conner but I found out later on that her nickname was Horse Head and she most definitely earned that nickname. She had a large head with reddish-brown hair. From hearing the many conversations about her, there's nothing she enjoys more than watching a hard, Black penis erupt.

I get up and go through my morning routine of brushing and flossing, I do two hundred pushups while listening to *Frankie Beverly* and *Maze* sing about *Happy Feelings*. Once the yard opens up, I head to the other end of the prison to catch my old work partner, Inmate Gene, before he goes to work. My timing was just right. I bump right into him by the Barber Shop.

"Inmate Gene, what's up brother?"

He looks up at me and says, "Helimite! They finally let you outta the box."

"Hell yeah, Gene. I beat the case. I was just back there under investigation."

"Yeah, I know because they had that dude Killer Miller in the medical infirmary for a while. He was fucked up but he wouldn't tell the police who he was fighting so they transferred him. He told me to tell you that it's a small world inside the Florida Prison system and that he will see you again."

I laughed and said, "Some people never learn. Check this out Gene. I need you to help me get my Medical Orderly job back for me. I have 25 natural dollars right now for you to make that happen."

He looked at me and said, "In my world money talks, Helimite."

"That's a deal, brother!" I pay him the 25 and get in the Barber Shop line.

14

I need a haircut and shave after being in confinement all that time. When my turn comes to get in the chair, I choose to get in Buck's chair. He's from Orlando. I ask him to cut me a Mike Tyson fade with a clean shave.

He tells me, "That's not regulation so if you want me to cut that, I charge three dollars."

I tell him, "No problem. I got you."

Hardee C.I. has filled to capacity and has a vibe of its own already going. Everybody that hustled when they were in society hustles when they enter the prison system. Nobody likes to have to call home and ask a family member or girlfriend for a money order so the hustles continue on the inside.

It's almost the end of September 1992 and my birthday, October 21st, is near so I need to make sure I have all my ducks in order for my birthday party. My partner, Gigolo and Uncle Willie always emphasized on celebrating whatever holidays and birthdays and any other events I considered worthy of a celebration. Even though this is prison, I programmed my mindset to be as if I'm on an all-male college campus. If you keep gazing at the razor wire and gun towers, you will trap your mindset into believing that you're just a slave in here with no way out of this modern-day plantation.

I get out of Buck's barber chair and look in the mirror. I'm so fresh and so clean, I give him three dollars and hit the door. I got released from confinement just in time to see the concrete being poured for the first basketball court. I notice a few brothers walking around with basketball rosters trying to build a team before a league started.

It's a beautiful day. The sun feels so good on my pale skin. All that time in that confinement cell has my skin complexion very light so I continue my walk out toward the softball outfield. There are inmates lying in the grass doing all kinds of stuff. To my left an inmate has a big, brown towel spread out playing poker. Since gambling was against the prison rules they had to come out here for a little bit more privacy.

I look to my right and had to chuckle to myself. That same karate class I noticed out here a month ago was still in session with them hot ass prison coats on. The lil short guy with a toothpick in his mouth barks out orders and corrects whatever wrong stance or movements they make. As I looked closer, the short guy instructor barking out orders looked familiar. At that moment it hit me who the instructor is. He's my new roommate, Mr. Bell.

I walk over toward the softball bleacher and sit down to watch the movement of the compound when all of a sudden the sound of a familiar voice breaks my chain of thought.

"Deli ham or turkey and cheese sandwiches on toast. One dollar!"

I turn my head to the left and see my main man Hobo selling sandwiches to three inmates talking shit, "No deals. One dollar a piece!"

I yell out, "Hobo, let me get two of them turkey and cheese sandwiches, my brother."

He looks at me, "Well I be damned. If it ain't my right-hand man, Helimite a.k.a. Mr. Telephone Man!"

"What you mean by 'Mr. Telephone Man'?"

"Man, everybody heard about how you almost beat Killer Miller to death with the phone receiver. You the reason every dorm has a phone list now – to keep the bullshit down about phone time." Hobo pauses and stares at me, "Damn Helimite, you need to get out there in the sun and get your color back. I almost didn't recognize you."

I laugh and say, "In due time I'll get out there and sweat a lil bit."

Hobo responds, "My homeboy gonna kill them boys out there in that field with them coats on."

I look toward the karate class, "Hell yeah. They trippin'. Ain't no way I'll be over there in a fake ass karate class. All them dudes out there just trying to keep other inmates off they ass. That's why they out in the open for everybody to see."

Hobo replies, "I can't speak for everybody but my homeboy who teaching the class…"

I interrupt, "The short guy teaching the class is my new roommate."

"You bullshittin' me," Hobo says.

"Naw, I'm fa real."

"Two fools in one room, huh? Well all I'm gonna say is that my homeboy is the most dangerous person I know with his hands and feet." Hobo pauses and stares at me, "You really don't know who your roommate is?"

"Yeah," I say, "Mr. Bell."

Hobo tilts his head to the side and responds, "Mike Bell was the World Champion in Taekwondo. He kicked ass all in Japan and the United States. He fucked up about twelve officers who tried to arrest him in Orlando for some bullshit. His nickname is The Lil Giant."

I'm processing all this information while Hobo gets my sandwiches together.

"All I have left is one turkey and cheese and one ham," Hobo says.

"Just give me the turkey and cheese sandwich, Hobo, I don't eat pork!"

Hobo asks, "You don't eat pork? What kinda negro you is? Let me guess, you Muslim?"

I reply, "No I'm not Muslim. I just decided to stop eating pork after reading an article on it in the newspaper."

"I bet yo Black ass grew up eating the pig every chance you got," Hobo teases.

"Yes I did but back then I didn't have a choice. I ate what my momma cooked and always went back for another plate."

Hobo laughs and gives me a handshake, "I know that's right!"

The prison intercom comes to life and announces that the yard is being called for count. "All inmates have ten minutes to report to your assigned dormitories."

15

Mike Bell is extremely quiet and clean. You couldn't ask for a better roommate. After about two weeks of being roommates, I started a conversation with him about how Michigan chose to start five Black freshmen on their basketball team and nicknamed them the "Fab 5" and how I couldn't wait for them to play Duke University. I don't remember how the conversation shifted to fighting but it did and Mike Bell asked me if I was interested in learning the art of Taekwondo. He got up and reached into his locker and pulled out a manila envelope full of newspaper articles with pictures of him holding up belts and trophies. He was letting me know that he was the real deal.

I tell him that I wouldn't mind learning the art but under one condition.

He looks at me and says, "What would that be, Helimite?"

"Teach me the art right here in our cell. I don't want everyone to see or know that I'm learning the art. Being out there in the field with a hot ass coat on for hours, I'm not interested in. And me knowing that everybody has an angle or a hustle, what you gon' charge me?"

Mike Bell scratches his head and responds, "If you would have asked me to train you I would have charged you a fee but I asked you if you wanted to learn it so there's no fee, Helimite a.k.a. Mr. Telephone Man."

We both erupt with laughter and a handshake to seal the deal. Every night from midnight to 3 a.m., Mr. Bell trained me in the art of Taekwondo fighting and defense. His training technique was very effective. Everything he taught me was taught using physical pain examples and demonstration. I quickly learned all of the pressure points of the human body that would make you scream like a pot of hot grits had been thrown in your face, your nuts, your eyes, ears, nose, throat and mouth.

Night after night I would train and execute what I had learned on Mr. Bell himself and if he didn't holler, I wasn't doing it right. I stayed at it night after night, throwing punches, blocking punches, thousands of kicks and knee lifts, how to defend myself in a knife situation. With all this new fighting knowledge along with the stuff I already did, it was going to be a sad day for whoever crossed that line and disrespected me.

After a long workout with Mike on Saturday night, we sat down and talked. Mike would take me all over the world telling me about all the people he defeated.

"You now the best thing about fighting, Helimite?" he asked.

"Naw, what is it?"

He answered, "The best thing about fighting is that there are no rules so how can you lose? You do what you must by any means necessary to stay alive in this institutional world."

"You dead right, Mike. I'll remember that, good brother!"

The next day I get up and take a shower at 6 a.m. and get dressed in my all-white medical uniform, put on some *Grey Flannel* cologne and hit the door for breakfast. My coworker, Inmate Gene did right by me in helping me get my job back. I am forever grateful even if it did cost me twenty-five more dollars.

Nurse Bracey was **still quiet as kept** with our arrangement for that kryptonite weed so business was booming. I never sold anyone anything. I let my homeboys handle that part. All I did was pick up money from my homeboy Damien out on the softball bleachers every Saturday. Damien was the little brother of my partner, Mark Oats, who died in the streets of Palm Beach County years back while I was locked up at Polk C.I. The least I could do is look after his little brother in prison.

My once professional relationship with Nurse Precious 27 had begun to grow into an unprofessional relationship and I was loving every minute of it. She wanted her office cleaned everyday by me so we could talk. I would flirt like crazy with her as long as no one was near. She talked all that talk about how good Latin women could cook and I would politely say, "I can't tell. Bring me a plate and let me be the judge."

She put her hands on her sexy ass hips, moved her hair out her face, tilted her head to the side and said, "Okay."

I told her I eat everything but pork and pussy. She put her hand over her mouth to hold her laughter in. Once it passed, she looked at me and says, "The lies you tell. You eat me like a cookie every time you see me walk by."

"What are you talking about?" I respond.

"Don't play dumb, Helimite. Why is your dick always hard when you come to clean for me?"

"Nurse Precious, I'm sorry to tell you this but that's my dick print on soft."

Her eyes widen with disbelief.

I tell her, "If you act right, I let you see what it looks like hard."

She looks me right in my eyes and says, "Get your freaky ass outta my office now, Helimite." She puts her right hand on my chest and pushes me toward the exit door. She felt on my chest muscles at the same time and I knew it was just a matter of time before I had this Brazilian chick with long flowing black hair caught up in the rapture of my love, as *Anita Baker* used to sing about.

I sweep and mop all the areas that needed it, gather all the trash in the building and take it outside to be dumped behind the kitchen. It was 10 a.m. and I wouldn't return to Medical until count time at noon. The two hours I had to myself, I normally go and talk to Nardo and Dr. Rock. Our conversations were always good and informative. Every time we saw each other, Dr. Rock and I would wrestle for at least thirty minutes. The funny part about it is that Dr. Rock had asthma and he would stop the wrestling match in the middle of the action to hit his asthma pump. Nardo was the look out. He would laugh at us. This was Stonybrook versus Ivey Green. I would tell Nardo, "You next, negro!"

His response was, "You ain't ready for Federal Gardens, young man!"

Neither of them knew I was training with Mr. Bell every night. Plus I'd never use the art on them anyway.

16

"Hey Helimite!"

I turn to see who is calling me and it's my homeboy, Butch, with a piece of paper in his hand walking toward me. Butch was 6'3", skinny as a toothpick, high yellow with wavy hair that he brushed constantly.

"What's up, Butch?"

"Hey man," he says. "We trying to get a Palm Beach basketball team together. You interested in playing?"

"Hell yeah. Who all you got so far?" I ask.

"Me and you. Not too many people here from Palm Beach or Ft. Lauderdale right now. Maybe the bus will bring a few more from down south this week."

"It's possible," I respond.

"Hey, Helimite!" Another voice I don't recognize calls out. I look to the right and this brother named Pepe Poole from Hollywood, Florida steps to me and asks, "You got here today?"

I respond, "Naw brother. I been here at Hardee. I was one of the first one hundred people at this prison. I work in Medical so I'm inside all the time."

"Oh shit," Pepe Poole says. "You got one of them good jobs!"

"Yeah, it's alright," I say.

"Well check this out Helimite, I'm trying to put a squad together for the new basketball league Hardee C.I. is starting next week," Pepe Poole comments.

"I already signed with my homeboy Butch," I say. "How many brothers you got so far?"

Pepe Poole answers, "Four with me included."

"Well we only have two. Are them boys you got, ballers?" I ask.

"Hell yeah," Pepe Poole says. "Broward County's finest."

"Well get with my homeboy Butch right here and y'all combine y'all rosters into one and decide on a name for the team."

Pepe Poole nods his head in agreement. "If the bus bring two more good ballers from Palm Beach, I will add them to the roster. All we need is a eight-man team to insure everyone gets a good amount of playing time. For now we have six."

Pepe Poole had his radio with him and the old school rap song *Planet Rock* had just come on.

Party people

Party people

Do you wanna get funky

Soul Sonic Force, do you wanna get funky

Just hit me

As the bass dropped, Pepe Poole broke into a pop and lock dance routine. I had met Pepe Poole down at the South Florida Reception Center on the basketball court, playing a game of horse. I can clearly remember him having the Midas touch from the three-point line and beyond.

Pepe Poole was around 6'1" and kind of on the heavy side but he could move around very well. Once *Planet Rock* went off I laughed and said, "Pepe Poole, we need a name for our team."

Pepe Poole looked at me, "Shit. How 'bout the Zulu nation?"

I reply, "The Zulu nation is the name of a well-respected African tribe."

Pepe Poole stares at me dead in my eyes and says, "We all from Africa and way the Zulu nation was kicking ass, I'm pretty sure I'm a descendent of that tribe. How 'bout you?"

I thought about it, laughed and say, "Hell yeah."

Butch chimes in and says, "I like it too."

The Zulu Nation, we became.

Our first practice went very well. The basketball chemistry was on fire. The funny thing about it was five out of the six people we had could slam dunk that basketball and with authority. We ended the practice with a huddle and some small talk. I reached in my pocket and pull out, what appears to the others, a hand rolled cigarette. Really, it was a fat ass joint. I fire it up. Four of us share it.

It's 6:30 p.m., a nice breeze is blowing and we have five super two radios on the same station listening to *Ain't Nothing But A G-Thang* by *Dr. Dre* and *Snoop Dogg*. We are good and high and shoot free throws for the next hour and jammin' while we shoot.

When the P.B.L. (Prison Basketball League) finally started, the Zulu Nation took the league by storm. We beat all thirteen teams twice, like they had slapped our momma's and we wanted revenge. We won all the holiday tournaments as well.

The prison bus continued to bring new inmates every week and all the other teams continued to draft better talent to try and stop our undefeated run. The Zulu Nation, at the time, was 36-0. Every time the female Recreation Director issued us any kind of winning certificate, she always typed in our team name as Z Nation. She refused to put 'Zulu' on any of our certificates. We didn't care because we were winning games and money every time the other teams felt like they had made an upgrade to their teams.

Things had become very clique-ish among the prison population especially the basketball teams. The Zulu Nation was still a Palm Beach and Ft. Lauderdale team. All the other teams weren't mixed. There was a Tampa Team, Miami Team, Polk County, Orlando Team and so forth.

I can't remember whose idea it was to start this county by county, one-game elimination basketball tournament. In the elimination tournament, you lose one game you're out of the tournament. The thing about this tournament was that the Recreation Department had nothing to do with it or any knowledge of the terms and conditions of said tournament. For each team to enter the tournament, there was a $100 entry fee. That money was being collected and held by Big Dickey, who is the canteen operator. We called him Big Dickey because he weighed over 300 pounds. The winner takes the whole pot, which ends up being $1,200.

The first round match ups were randomly chosen. I can't compare the skillset or talent level in the prison to any NBA team but I can put some of the teams up against college level athletes. Hardee C.I. had some ballers. For the money everybody had on their A-game, the only problem we had was finding three neutral referees to call the games. All twelve team coaches had to be in agreement on who the referees would be.

The tournament started at 9:00 a.m. on Saturday and would end with the championship game on Sunday at 6:00 p.m., weather permitting. In my opinion, the only teams that even stood a chance against the Zulu Nation was Polk County, St. Petersburg, and Miami squads. These games were so packed, hyped, and intense, the officers at Hardee didn't even attempt to get courtside to monitor any of these games. And I couldn't blame them for fear of losing their life in that atmosphere. It was smarter to be outside of that circle of inmates than smack dab in the middle of it.

The Zulu Nation didn't play until after lunch, 2 p.m., against the Orlando Finest. These brothers had some of the deadliest three-point shooters at the prison and a center everybody had nicknamed Baby Shaq. All the teams that were in the tournament were in attendance to watch game one of the elimination process. It was Polk County against Pensacola. I ordered eight frozen jungle juices for my team to have while we watched the game and fired up two joints and passed them around. My weed connect had held true with me and I was making good money and having it sent home to my sister once I accumulated too much.

Nardo and Dr. Rock walk up beside me and said, "Damn. These boys ballin' this morning."

I shake my head in agreement and commented, "For that twelve-hundred-dollar pot, you'd be balling too."

They both shake their heads in agreement. Dr. Rock goes on to say, "Helimite, one of your homeboys from Stonybrook got killed yesterday."

I turn to face him and ask, "Who?"

He responds, "A brother named Magill."

"Damn," I say. "I know who you talking about. Who they said killed him?"

Dr. Rock says, "Nobody mentioned anything yet."

"Damn! Shit crazy in Palm Beach right now," I comment.

"Sure is," Nardo responds. "Another young brother who lived over by Suncoast got killed too."

"What was his name?" I ask.

"Teddy Donald," Nardo answers.

"Teddy Donald," I repeat in disbelief. "That was my main man since Lincoln Elementary School. We used to fish together all the time. That was my best friend Sam's cousin. Who killed Teddy and why? He was just a cool ass player player. He wasn't into the thug life stuff. He was into women," I said.

I'm still trying to process what was happening in Palm Beach County. You would think that with all the time they gave my cousin and I for murder, it would discourage others from committing violent crimes. I am sitting here in Hardee C.I. with a 55-year sentence not knowing the day or hour I will ever see free society again. I need to call home and talk to Sam, Vell, and Charlie Wine. I hope my little sister will run a three-way call for me later.

The basketball game ends with Polk County being victorious.

I head to my dorm with heavy thoughts of Magill and Teddy on my mind. My weed high was completely blown! I lie on my bunk and begin to pray,

> *"Father, in the name of Jesus, I pray for peace and love to flow in Palm Beach County. I pray that justice is served on the people who killed Teddy and Magill and that you comfort their loved ones during this time of grief. In Jesus' name I pray. Amen."*

The murder rate was on a steady rise in my hometown. I felt relieved to know my older brother, Magic, had decided to return to Linden, New Jersey to live after getting caught up in the alley on S avenue with the police.

They arrested him for being in Charlie Wine's house where

cocaine was being sold.

17

The intercom comes to life in the dorm, announcing that count is clear and for all inmates to get ready for chow. The police never called it breakfast, lunch, or dinner. It was always announced as chow like they were feeding livestock or something. When they finally release my dorm for lunch, I go straight to Medical to make my rounds. Without a doubt, the Medical Department was my home away from home. The air conditioning, the homecooked meals from Nurse

Precious 27, and all the other staff were more than enough to put my soul at peace whenever times got hard.

Once I enter the building I find out immediately that Inmate Gene is in the building cleaning or pretending to. What I didn't know was that Medical had hired a new medical orderly. I ran into him in the back hallway, mopping the floors. He looked at me and I held his stare and said, "What's up brother? I'm Helimite," and I reach out to shake his hand.

He responds, "I'm Duck."

"Duck?!" I question.

He says, "Yeah but don't let the nickname fool you."

"Where you from, Duck?" I ask.

He answers, "Ft. Lauderdale."

I nod my head and tell him that I'm from Palm Beach.

Duck was 6'2" and was as black as 12 midnight with an all-white uniform on. He sported a big boy gold chain with diamonds all in his lion head medallion, a pinky ring full of diamonds and a Movado watch. He had on some brand-new white Charles Barkley's on with, what appeared to be, a black gator skin belt. The brother was clean and was modeling these prison clothes to the fullest. I'm pretty sure he paid Inmate Gene top dollar to be up in here.

"Welcome aboard, bro," I tell him and keep it moving. I head down the hall to Nurse Precious 27's office, knock on the door and walk in.

"Good afternoon, Nurse Precious. I'm here to clean your office. I clean everything but windows."

She laughs and says, "Yeah, right!"

I reach for some latex gloves, pull them on and leave to go to the caustic closet for a spray bottle with disinfectant in it and a clean rag to work with. When I arrive back, the new orderly was leaving her front door.

I enter her office and say, "So you met the new orderly?"

"Yes," she answers, "and I have politely told him you were taking care of all my cleaning needs and then he left."

"That's cool," I say.

I begin to wipe down the counters, shelves, and anything else to kill time. I brush up against Nurse Precious every time the opportunity presented itself and she never objected to my flirtatious tactics. Before I finished, she told me she cooked a Latin dish of chicken, rice, tomatoes, jalapenos, onions and olives with a piece of homemade banana bread for dessert.

"Don't let any staff see you eating it," she tells me.

I promised her that I wouldn't and asked her where it was located.

She responded, "On the bottom shelf of the refrigerator in a brown bag."

I head toward the break room to heat up this home cooked Latin meal that Nurse Precious 27 had so kindly prepared. When I pull the bag out of the fridge and look inside, there's enough food for two people but there was no way I was sharing this with Inmate Gene or the new guy, Duck. I take enough out to eat for now. I have a basketball game at 2 p.m. and I don't need to play on a full stomach.

I stick the paper plate in the microwave for two minutes and walk away from the break room until the food is heated. I come back in and smash the plate like the police was chasing me. I wash it down with some water and leave the medical building to get dressed for my game. We play Orlando Finest and I have an hour before the 2:00 tip off. I do my pregame ritual – take a shit, shower, and smoke half a joint and put my radio on a rap station until game time.

We already had a defense plan in place to stop Brent, their deadliest shooter, with the double team every time he touches the ball and let the rest of the team try to win it without Brent's 20-point average. Our game plan worked and we eliminated the Orlando squad. The Tampa squad was up next. The Zulu Nation blew them out, 60 to 40.

We had advanced to the championship game that was set for last yard at 6 p.m. We would play the winner between the Miami Boys and Polk County. Polk clearly had the better talent in that game but better talent doesn't necessarily win in prison, especially the big money games. Whatever team has the biggest heart to fight, and I do mean fight, wins these games and that's how it went. The Miami Boys began fouling the Polk County boys so hard, it wasn't even basketball anymore and Polk County knew it was time to tuck their tails and that, they did. One by one they quit after being fouled in a way that was unnecessary so the stage had been set for the Zulu Nation to play the Miami squad, 6:00 primetime.

I call a team meeting before hand to game plan and to give our ride-or-die homeboys a list of needs and must-haves for the game when 5:30 rolled around. The Zulu Nation showed up with 13 super-two radios. We sat them down at half court all tuned in on the same station as we began to warm up with a variety of dunks, with me hollering our war chant, "Face! The Nation! Zulu Nation!"

The game began with the Miami Boys trying to match up with us in a man to man defense, which was a bad decision. We were up 12 to 2 and gaining momentum. I had 8 of our 12 points and the Miami Boys best player, Jolly, insisted on guarding me the rest of the game. Jolly was the same height, same build. We could easily pass for twins except I looked better. Me and Jolly never once spoke to each other and I saw him every day at the pull-up bar and dip bar. From the moment I saw him, I knew we would be competing against each other in something sooner or later.

Jolly tried to manhandle me, defensively, in order to keep the ball out of my hands but I push him to the side and slash down the lane as Butch bounce passed the ball to me. As I rose up to dunk on whoever was in my way, somebody knocked me clean out the air like we were playing football.

I had to use both of my hands to break my fall. When I hit the ground the crowd went, "Ohhhhhh!"

I turn my head to see who had fouled me like that and there stood Jolly with a smirk on his face. The ref had blown the whistle and called it a foul. I got up, clapped my hands, and said, "Good foul. Let's play ball y'all." I shoot my first free throw and miss. I back away from the free throw line to gather myself and I ask the score table how many fouls I had. The score table answers, "You have two fouls, Helimite."

Before I can shoot the other free throw, Jolly goes to the score table, grabs the score book and rips it up completely. He looks at me and says, "You ain't got no fouls now, Helimite. We from the bottom of the map, negro. Talk don't scare us."

At that point, I had already made up my mind to teach Jolly some manners for the way he had just fouled me. I am really going to punish his ass now. I call a time out, huddle the squad up, talking loud and clear, "Stay focused fellas.

We gon' win this money. Stay focused. All that was just a front."

I tell the rest of the Zulu Nation to be on point because I was going to knock Jolly's ass out within the next five minutes. I am so glad I had instructed our homeboys to bring all the knives and pipes to the game tonight. I felt in my spirit that something might pop off so the Zulu Nation was ready for war. I began to chant, "Zulu," and the rest of the team and fans would answer, "Nation!"

I head back to the free throw line to shoot. Swoosh. This shot stood true and was nothing but net.

We were playing man to man and Jolly was still guarding me and I was guarding him as well. Jolly ran down the court on offense without the ball. I left him open enough to receive the ball so I could flip his ass if he tried to go to the hoop. As soon as his team mate passed the ball to him, he passed it back like it was a hot potato. One of his team mates, McDuffy, shot the ball and was fouled. We line up at the free throw line so that McDuffy could get his two shots. Jolly was right beside me as the free throw went right through the net. The score was 13 to 3.

When McDuffy shot his second free throw, it was way off. I turned to my left to box Jolly out. He was so focused on trying to get that rebound, he never saw my right fist headed toward his throat. All the radios on the sideline that the Zulu Nation had brought were all booming the hit song *whoop there it is, whoop there it is…* Hearing that song was like a signal that this would be the best opportunity to teach Jolly some manners. Once I connected, he gasped for air while reaching for his throat but I could care less. I was already headed for his nut sack with my right fist delivering a blow to smash any future kids he might want to make. All this took place in three seconds. Jolly was on the ground now and it was easy for me to pound on his ass. The whole court had bum rushed like someone had hit the winning shot at a college game.

I punch Jolly in the face. Somebody punched me in the back of my head. As I turn to see who it was, Nardo had already erased the dude from the spot with a clothesline blow. There were too many people on the court to recognize anyone else. I heard one familiar voice, Mark Oats' little brother Damien say, "Helimite you can get up when you ready. We got you surrounded with knives."

I say, "Okay," and raise up off the concrete. I get to my feet and move off the court and on to the grass. I look around the court, there was fighting going on everywhere and the police were nowhere to be found. The P.A. system sounds off, "The yard is closed. All inmates report to your dorm." The message repeats over and over but it was a waste of breath.

I spot the dude who had punched me in the back of the head while I was on the ground. To my surprise the new orderly, Duck, was connecting blows to his head causing him to stumble backwards. He was trying not to fall because if he did there would be many boots on his head. I turn to my right and see two guys with hats down low, whooping Officer Doo Doo Brown's ass and going in his pockets and taking his wallet. This is my first prison riot so I was unsure of what happens next.

Nardo says, "Helimite, we gonna walk you to your dorm. Lock down. Clean yourself up if need be.

I nod my head, a little shook, "Okay bro. Let's go."

I moved with my home team to the dorm. The officer pops the door to let me in and immediately runs down to the plexiglass window to ask me what is going on out there.

I tell him, "I'm not sure sir but it's a whole lot of fighting going on out there. What for, I'm not sure but for the record, remember my face and name."

He said, "Okay," and I went upstairs to lockdown.

While wondering how all this shit would play out, Mr. Bell came in ten minutes later. He asked me if I was okay and I responded that I was fine. He went on to say,

"There's a lot of blood everywhere on that basketball court and sidewalks. Security wasn't ready for nothing like this. At least three of them got beat up real bad. I'm pretty sure they gonna have off duty officers and officers from other prisons to come help restore order and when they get here, anybody who was involved gon' get their ass whooped all the way to confinement. All we can do is wait now, Helimite."

About two hours later, at least 30 officers entered our dorm with dogs and cans of mace. The three officers that got beat up went from cell to cell telling whoever was in the cell to come to the door so they could look them in the face. Even though this riot started about a basketball game, once a riot starts it's an open door to do whatever you want – snatch somebody's jewelry, break into the prison store – it's just like riots in free society but confined to one area and no fire bombs. If you're a known asshole corrections officer, you are at the top of the list to get beat the hell up.

When the three officers get to my cell and ask Mr. Bell and I to step to the door, I almost laughed when I saw the knots on Doo Doo Brown's face and all the dried blood on his shirt. His eyes were so big looking into our face, he probably still couldn't believe he had got his ass kicked by some inmates. He couldn't even identify me and Mr. Bell and they ordered us to return to our bunks as they moved to the next cell. I guess I dodged a bullet.

18

The following day the prison was on lock down. Mr.
Bell still had to go to the kitchen at 4 a.m. because the prison
still had to eat. At 8 a.m. I was told to get dressed and was
escorted to Medical for work. When I arrive at the building
all the medical staff was asking me what had happened the
day before. I played dumb and said I was in the dorm asleep
when the riot kicked off so I had no details on what had
actually happened.

I begin my cleaning duties. Once I reach Nurse Precious 27's office she lit up like a light the moment she laid eyes on me. She stopped pecking at her computer and got up from her desk. She looked outside her door to the left and to the right to confirm that the halls were empty then she gave me a hug and kissed me on the lips. She did it so fast that she caught me completely off guard. The way her nurse scrubs hugged her body and how her long hair fell down her back excited me. Her glasses sat on the bridge of her nose and made her look like a sexy librarian and her pink lipstick made her lips look plump and juicy.

I asked her in a curious tone, "What was that for?"

She responds, "We received phone calls at home that there had been a riot at the prison and a lot of stabbing had taken place. All I could think about was you."

I look in her eyes and respond, "Really?"

She moves her hair out of her face and says, "Yes, really, Helimite! You're the only inmate I have love for."

I take a step back to look down the hallways, from left to right. It is empty. I ask, "So, you love me?" as I grab her hand and pull her body close to me.

She looks at me and giggles, "No, silly. I have love for you but I'm not in love with you."

"Well I need to see what I can do about that," I say with a crooked grin on my face.

She slaps me on my shoulder and says, "I'm being serious right now, Helimite,"

"I am too," I respond.

She looks down and her voice diminishes to a whisper, "I was worried if you were safe and sound."

I pull her even closer and tell her, "Well, I was worried if I would ever get the opportunity to taste your tongue and suck on them lips."

She blushes and replies, "Which lips, Helimite?"

"Both," I say and she beams a wide smile at me.

"Don't threaten me with a good time especially when it's impossible to get nasty with you inside this prison," Nurse Precious scolds.

"Nurse Precious, that's not true! We can care for and about each other and still be careful if you're really serious about letting me explore every part of your body. I have a plan, and a perfect spot to make it happen."

"Okay then, let's hear it Helimite."

I explain, "When everyone leaves for lunch at noon walk down the hall to the X-ray room on the right."

"I don't have a key to that X-ray room," Nurse Precious 27 says.

"Don't worry about the key. I have one. When you're ready for that day and moment, the door will already be opened. All you'll have to do is walk in and close the door. The X-ray room is only used one day out of the week and that's Monday. The rest of the week, it's closed."

"How did you manage to get a key, Helimite?"

I respond, "If I tell you that, I will have to kill you so to avoid any violence, I'll remain **quiet as kept** on that one."

Nurse Precious 27 shakes her head from side to side and laughs, "Okay, let me think about it."

I nod my head in agreement.

She says, "Now tell me what started the riot."

I told her everything leaving out all the parts I played in it. That would be too much information.

Hardee C.I. stayed locked down for three days straight before they opened the yard back up. Security decided they would make their presence felt. At least thirty officers walked the yard, talking shit and pat searching inmates for weapons. Even with the thirty officers on display, it couldn't stop and wouldn't stop over 1,700 angry inmates if they decided to riot again.

I walked over toward the canteen to buy me a pint of butter pecan ice cream. I handed the canteen operator a five-dollar bill and waited for my pint and three-dollar change. The canteen operator gave me exactly six-hundred and three dollars back. I looked down in his window and saw the 300-pound Big Dickey standing there. He said, "I gave the Miami Boys 600 and you 600 since the game never actually finished with a winner.

I told Dickey, "Okay bro. That sounds about right."

I put the money in my pocket and started toward my dorm. From what I had seen and heard, everyone on my team was safe and sound. To God be the glory as my mother would always say. I had decided to stay away from the basketball court for a while and concentrate on making my money. I couldn't go to the Law Library yet because Hardee still hadn't built one so I couldn't research if any new case law had come out yet pertaining to illegal sentences.

I hid inside the Medical building, working all the time, going to the dorm after dinner to shower, smoke a joint and write letters. Late night, I trained with Mr. Bell. I wasn't receiving a whole lot of mail lately. With the mail I was sending out, I should be receiving quite a few letters in the near future.

19

With my birthday only a week away now I had carefully planned a party. Nurse Bracey was still my go-to person for anything I needed that was illegal and I paid her accordingly for her services. I had close to a pound of weed in the ceiling of the medical building. I would bring out only two ounces at a time to serve the compound. There were still rumors out that the Department of Corrections was establishing a urinalysis testing program set up by Tallahassee to randomly test inmates for weed and cocaine.

Me, personally, I was smoking like a Navajo chief while the coast was still clear to smoke. I had no idea how this testing would affect my bottom line, making sales, so all I could do was wait. I kept Hardee C.I. flooded with the biggest prison dime bags they have ever seen. We used three *Chapstick* caps to make a dime bag with back then. You could easily make fifteen dollars off my dime bags.

I spoke with the compound plumber and convinced him to steal and sell me a pipe chase key for twenty dollars cash. Access to the pipe chase gave me a solid spot to hide whatever I wanted to inside my dorm. I had already made two five-gallon buckets of grapefruit juice wine and decided to add a flavor twist to it by adding four bags of *Jolly Rancher* candy to each bucket.

The recipe for each bucket was seven pounds of white sugar, four bags of *Jolly Ranchers* candy, four spoons of baking yeast, two gallons of water, three gallons of grapefruit juice, and one box of raisins. Let it cook for fourteen days straight inside that hot ass pipe chase.

To make sure the wine smell didn't get out, I applied Ben Gay to the walls around the pipe chase every day. I worked in Medical so obtaining Ben Gay was nothing major. I had twenty-five joints rolled, had Hobo hook up some beef fried rice, enough of it to feed at least twenty people that we heated up on top of our room heaters. I had Nurse Bracey bring me three sixteen-ounce *Sprite* bottles inside her lunch bag that was full of *Tanqueray* gin. This was what I would be drinking along with my main circle of people who made my business run like clockwork.

My dorm, 2A, had turned into a powerhouse dorm at the prison. We had a solid breed of dudes in there from every county in Florida. We had a poker game in 2A that had at least three grand in the pot every day. Table stake was two hundred dollars to get in. Gangster Mud from Miami. Cuban BeBe from Tampa. Bay Bay from Broward. Black Jack from

St. Pete. Stan O from Orlando and Helimite from Palm Beach. We were at that table so much together, gambling against each other that with time we all became a family that networked to make our dorm and Hardee a much more tolerable place.

My birthday party at the dorm would kick off after the 4 p.m. count on October 21, 1992. It started for me at midnight. I thanked the Lord for allowing me to see another year. I thanked him for my health and strength in Jesus' name and fired up a joint of that kryptonite. Mr. Bell didn't smoke but he did drink. I poured up two cups of the *Tanqueray* and added orange juice and let my radio, that was tuned in to the quiet storm, take me down memory lane.

Ready For The World was singing *Let Me Love You Down* and I was so high I could hear every instrument and vocal in that song. What was I doing the first time I heard this song? I close my eyes and go to that place in time where I was always free, safe, laughing, and clowning as a young, immature teenager. My Lincoln Elementary school crush, Nicole V. had grown up to be a beautiful Red Bone with long, wavy hair. It had been four years since I had seen her and when I did lay eyes on her again, it was at Twin Lakes homecoming game and she, of course, was the homecoming queen.

I was stunned by her beauty. My homeboy Vell punched me in the arm and said, "Helimite, close your mouth cause ain't no way you can pull that."

I tell Vell, "I know her. I used to play in her hair in the fifth grade and she always used to tell the teacher on me. Her name Nicole."

"Fifth grade," Vell says. "Helimite I bet that girl don't and won't even remember you if you was standing right in front of her."

"Yeah, Vell, you probably right." But in the back of my mind I was hoping and wishing for that opportunity. Three weeks later, without even knowing, my homeboy

Reggie Washington started dating a girl named Heather. At the time she was best friends with Nicole. I was at Reggie's house while he was on the phone with Heather.

During that conversation I said, "Reggie, ask Heather do she have a girlfriend that's single and not ugly.

He says, "No!" Then says, "Wait a minute. Her girl Nicole broke up with Lorenzo a few days ago so she single and very pretty. Smart too."

I asked Reggie to let me speak to Heather and he handed me the phone. I asked Heather what was Nicole's last name and when she told me I went silent for a minute, gathered my thoughts and said, "Tell her Helimite, Reggie's best friend, wants to meet her. How 'bout y'all meet me and Reggie at the Twin City Mall on Saturday night. We can get some of that good ole caramel popcorn with the pecans in it and watch that new movie, *Krush Groove* while we there."

"I'm down, Helimite, but I gotta call her and see if she available on Saturday night," Heather says.

"Ok. See what you can do," I tell her.

The next day, Friday, I received word from Reggie that we would be double dating that Saturday night just as I had planned it. I went home that evening, put one of my Jam Pony Express tapes on and washed my money-green-four-door Chevy Impala and vacuumed the inside. I was looking forward to going to the movies with Nicole mainly because I knew her but she didn't know me. Heather had told her my nickname Helimite. Nicole only knew me by my government name.

When Saturday night came and we all met in the parking lot at Twin City Mall, I introduced myself as Helimite. After the movie, I explained to her how I had been crazy about her for years and she was puzzled at when and where all of that had taken place. When I finally told her that I sat behind her in the fifth grade in Mr. Walker's class and used to play in her hair until she told on me, she screamed, "Oh my gosh, Vincent McDaniels!"

"Yes! The one and only," I respond.

She asks, "When did they start calling you Helimite?"

"In the seventh grade," I say. "A lot has changed since the fifth grade, Nicole."

"Yes, it has and you have built quite a terrible reputation for yourself," Nicole declares.

"Don't believe all the rumors, Nicole." I defend myself, "When trouble comes my way, which seems to be more often now…" I reached out to hold her in my arms, pulling her to me with my back up against the car.

She put her hands on my chest and says, "Don't try and kiss me, Vincent McDaniels. I don't know where your lips have been. I've done my homework on you and all the information I gather said you a ho-ho-ho."

"If you even believed any of the stuff you heard, you wouldn't be here now in my arms." Before she could respond, my beeper goes off.

"Who's beeping you? One of your girlfriends?" Nicole looks at me sideways as I turn to look at my beeper.

"Nope. This is business," I tell her while putting my beeper back in my pocket.

"I don't know where Reggie and Heather went in my car," Nicole says.

"Not too far. Just far enough for some privacy. Get in my car and chill 'til they roll back through." I crank the car, turn on the air conditioning, turn the radio on and a new song by *Ready For The World* is on. *Let Me Love You Down* is playing. I'm looking at her. She's looking at me and I start playing in her hair, listening to the lyrics of the song.

She tells me that she enjoyed the movie and thanks me for the invite.

"No problem," I pause, "Are you going to the *New Edition, Force MD's,* and *Cherelle* concert at the West Palm Beach Auditorium next week?"

She answers, "Yes."

I move to grab her hand and say, "I'll be there too. We should hook up."

"Maybe. Let me think about it," she says with a side glance at me.

I say, "Cool. Can you at least give me the seven digits so I can call and check on you from time to time?"

She tells me her number. I write it down and I watch her get out of the car to get in her car with Heather. I'm kind of mad because I didn't even get a chance to kiss her. Reggie hops in and says, "Whassup with you, Helimite?"

"Nothing, bro," I answer.

"Well did you get to know her better?" Reggie asks.

"Yeah, I did. She playing hard right now but I'll get her, Reggie. I didn't even get a kiss!"

Reggie laughed and said, "You know girls don't kiss on the first date."

"Man, that's only TV," I say.

He laughs again and says, "I can't tell."

"I'll catch up with her at the New Edition concert," I tell Reggie.

20

Thanksgiving had come and gone. The kitchen hadn't put any effort into making the meal worthwhile. They served us sliced turkey, mashed potatoes and gravy, cranberry sauce, green beans, and two bread rolls. I wasn't too concerned because the Medical Department always brought homecooked food for every holiday. Duck and I and Inmate Gene ate very well because we had to clean up the break room after every party. And the food that was left over, we could eat for two days. The women took care of us like family and we remained **quiet as kept** through it all.

We kept the Medical Department extremely clean so no one could ever say anything about how much time we spent inside the building. This time of year always seemed to fly by and a very big part of me yearned to be home for Christmas. It was important for a lot of inmates to get a visit from a family member on Christmas day but I never wanted a visit on Christmas. That day should be spent at home around loved ones, not on the road standing in a long ass line trying to get inside the prison.

A memo had been put up in every dorm that this would be the last year that the Department of Corrections would be giving every inmate in the Florida prison system five dollars cash for Christmas. If that wasn't bad enough, the memo also stated that effective 1 February 1993, the Department of Corrections would be removing all cash money from the prison system and providing all inmates with a cashless card, also known as a prison debit card. If your family or friends sent you money, it was added to a card with your name and prison number on it. This was going to have a huge effect on all illegal activities funded by the almighty dollar. I had close to a three-month time frame to rake in as much cash as possible.

I already controlled the drug trade at Hardee C.I. To be prepared for the five free dollars that the prison gave every inmate, on December 22nd, I had my people, the Zulu Nation rather, sack up three ounces of nothing but five-dollar bags, which is one chap stick cap of weed. I instructed my workers to let the inmates credit a five-dollar bag until they received their five dollars from the prison, which would be handed out like clockwork on December the 24th.

The State of Florida felt like the money would recycle itself back to them once we spent the five dollars in the canteen but this year was going to be different. I wasn't in the mindset to get this money, I was in the mindset of trappin' the money. That's a big difference in a hustler's world.

When you trap money, it can't go anywhere because it's trapped. My people giving out that credit two days before the five-dollar payout was the trap process. Now in order to turn all them fives into bigger bills, all the inmates coming back from the visiting park with large bills from their family and friends needed those big bills broke down into change. You need change for $100, it costs! I give you $90 for the $100 or you can just buy some drugs and the money will change itself.

I thought about throwing a big Christmas party in my dorm but after all that happened at my birthday party, I decided against it. The two five-gallon buckets of wine with the *Jolly Rancher* flavor proved to be too much for the dorm. Since I made it, I had to sample it before anyone else and it had a California Cooler type taste going on. It was extremely strong yet smooth. The *Jolly Rancher* candy was nothing but more sugar with different flavors. The more sugar you have in the wine has an impact on the proof of the alcohol. The yeast eats the sugar. If I had to guess, I'd say that those buckets were around 50 proof after two weeks of cooking.

By 9 p.m., the night of my party, there had already been two fights over nothing. The guys were drunk, throwing up, and throwing punches. We had the volume turned down on the TV because everyone's radios were tuned to the same station. I had passed out all the pre-rolled joints right at 6 p.m. and had the wine served at 7. The food barely got touched due to everybody chasing a free high. To keep things from getting worse, we removed the last four out of ten gallons of wine, putting it back inside the pipe chase. I could sell those four gallons for $60 cash.

I remember a few dudes trying to rape this young white boy I had nicknamed 90210 because he looked just like one of those young, rich White kids on that TV show, *Beverly Hills 90210*. I can still hear the slap that landed on

90210's face. It was loud but the voice that came behind it was even louder. It was Greedy Man and he was doing a couple of life sentences so he wasn't going anywhere soon. He would die in prison so Greedy Man was looking for a man-wife.

The radios were jammin' *Wreckx-N-Effect's* hit, *All I Wanna Do Is Zoom a Zoom Zoom Zoom in a poom poom, just shake your rump.* I could clearly hear Greedy Man say, "Get naked, cracker! And you better not shit on me." There was one more dude in the room in case 90210 wanted to resist. Apparently 90210 was moving way too slow so Greedy Man punched him in the stomach.

I entered the room and said, "Whassup gangsters."

They both look at me and say, "Whassup Big Dog. Happy Birthday."

I respond, "Bet that up. I need for y'all to do me a favor."

"What you need, Helimite?" Greedy Man asks.

"Leave this White boy alone. He owes me way too much money for y'all to run him to Protective Management plus he gonna point y'all out for rape and y'all are going to Hardee County Jail. So, all I want for my birthday is for y'all to leave this White boy alone. If you that horny, go to my room and I'll give y'all two of them new *Playboy* magazines I have. It's safe sex and you don't have to worry about the magazine shitting on your dick."

They busted out laughing and agreed. "Helimite, my bad dog. I didn't know you had the cracker on your books."

"Greedy Man you know I'm **quiet as kept** with my business so we good, dog."

They both left the room. I stood there alone with 90210 and said, "That was a close one, huh? You were about to give up your virginity tonight."

His face was red. His eyes were wide with fear as he began to cry. I tell him, "Save them tears for another day. Do you believe in God?"

He nods his head up and down.

I said, "Ok then. Repeat after me. Father, in the name of Jesus, I thank you for your grace and mercy and I thank you for using Helimite to stop them fools from raping me tonight. In Jesus' name, amen."

I tell 90210 to get himself together and that from now on he works for me. I continue, "If anybody tries to put down on you, tell them you Helimite people."

"And what do you want in return?" 90210 asks.

"Nothing," I answer, "God got me!" and I walk out the room.

A Christmas party was out of the question!

21

Things were moving along like clockwork. Me and

the new orderly, Duck, had gotten tight. He had a few chicks

in Medical that was clearly digging him but he acted like he

was oblivious to it all. I decided to have a talk with him in

one of the medical isolation cells they used when an inmate

had something contagious. We had turned this one cell into

our hang-out spot away from everybody.

"Duck," I say, "You from Ft. Lauderdale?"

He says, "Yeah."

"Do you know Pana Cat or Big Shorty?" I ask.

"I heard those names before but never met them. Why?" Ducks responds.

"Just asking bro. Them solid dudes that I know and they live down there. Check this, Duck. It don't take a genius to figure out it's a few women up here that like you."

He smiles and says, "Really."

"Bro. Real talk. Why you up here?" I ask him.

Duck answers, "To work and chill in this air condition."

"So, you don't want no pussy or head?" I ask.

"Naw. I'm straight. I'm not gonna lose my visitation messing with these women. My lady comes to visit me every Saturday and Sunday." Duck says it with deep sentiment.

"Good for you," I say, "So you just up here modeling with them tight ass pants and shirt on. These women wanna fuck but you wanna model. How much time you got?"

"None of your business, Helimite! You do your time your way and I'll do mine how I see fit."

"Okay, Duck. If nothing else, do me one favor really two."

"What's that, Helimite?" Duck asks.

I answer, "First, I may need you to watch out for me sometime while we at work. And second, stop wearing that stank ass cologne up here."

He laughed and said, "That's *Obsession*. I know it don't stank."

"Well, you must be musky as hell then," I tease.

"Helimite, you got me fucked up."

"No, I don't. I have never gotten high with you. Your square ass probably don't even smoke." I tell him.

"Fire it up and see. It's my turn to laugh now," Duck says.

"Not in this building," I tell him, "I'll catch up with you on the yard one day this week."

"How much an ounce sell for at Hardee?" Duck asks.

I answer, "$500 last I heard." Even though I'm the plug, I have to protect my identity.

Duck looks at me, "I'm interested in buying two ounces."

I'm not really sure what Duck's angle is but I'm not concerned about these two ounces because I have already trapped the Christmas money that the State's given out. The two ounces he is purchasing may be for his personal use or for his homeboys to establish a hustle. I ask, "Well, when you want them two ounces?"

"Christmas day, if possible," Duck answers.

"I'll talk to somebody for you."

Duck nods his head and says, "I have a thousand in cash already."

"I believe you Duck. Just hold up and let me see if it's available."

We both leave and go our separate ways. I take all the trash out and dump it behind the kitchen. I pull off the latex gloves I had on and trash them as well. It's hot as hell out here today plus that cow pasture right next to the prison had the air smelling foul.

I start walking toward my dorm when I hear somebody call my name. To my surprise, it's my old roommate Hollywood. I speak, "How you doing, Hollywood?"

He has those *Blues Brothers* shades on and says, "I'm okay, Helimite. Shake my hand."

I reach out to shake his hand and he hands me something and says, "Christmas ain't Christmas without no snow!" and walks off.

I call out, "It's too hot to be dreaming of a white Christmas, Hollywood!" I laugh and head on to my dorm. When I reach my room, I go in my pocket to see what Hollywood had given me. It was at least two grams of powder cocaine. Cocaine sells for a hundred dollars a gram and he had given me two or better. He must have a lot of this stuff. Now I can understand why that quiet ass Hollywood was always sniffing and sounding like he had a cold. He was snorting cocaine the whole time and I never had a clue.

It's Christmas Eve and my radio is playing *What Do The Lonely Do At Christmas*. I get up, reach into my locker and grab my phone book. I walk down the flight of stairs and take the phone off the hook. I look through my book for my soul sister's number. I hope she's home. If she's there, I'll be able to get up to speed on what's really happening back home.

OPERATOR: How may I help you?

ME: Yes Operator, I would like to make a collect call to number 561-848-2322.

OPERATOR: And your name sir?

ME: Helimite

OPERATOR: I'm sorry. Can you pronounce that for me again?

ME: Yes, I can. Heli like in a helium balloon and Might like I might be going home soon. Helimite.

OPERATOR: Ok. Please hold.

A few seconds later I hear the operator telling Shorty Brown, "I have a collect call from Helimite. Do you accept the charges?"

I hear Shorty Brown clearly say, "Yes, I do"

"Helimite! What's going on with you, soul brother?"

"Nothing much. Just doing time and maintaining. How are you?" I ask.

"All over the place, Helimite. I'm about to start nursing school in a few months and I can't wait."

"That's good news, Shorty Brown. You still going to visit my cousin at Glades Correctional Institution?"

"No. I have way too much going on for that right now. We still cool though. I have somebody I'm dating seriously right now anyway."

I ask, "Who you dating?"

"Marcus!" she states.

"From downtown?" I ask.

"Yeah," she responds. "His nickname is Ten."

"That's him. I didn't know you knew him, soul sister. I know everybody that is somebody. Tell him I said whassup."

"Okay. I will," she says.

"So how is the rest of the family?" I call Shorty Brown my soul sister because she skipped school every day during my murder trial to make sure that she was there to support me and her best friend, Beth.

"Everyone is doing fine. Beth's cousin, Rhonda, is over here with me."

"Tell Rhonda I said hello. What y'all doing?" I ask.

"We getting ready to go to a Christmas Eve party at Club La Riviera." Shorty Brown answers.

"Damn, I wish I could go with y'all instead of being locked up with all these hard heads that's always trying to exercise game. Where Beth at?" I ask.

"She at home getting dressed. She's going too."

I ask Shorty Brown, "Can you do a three-way call for me so I can talk to her? I don't have the new number."

"Okay," Shorty Brown says with reluctance, "I'll call but don't start all that arguing!"

My 55-year sentence had brought my relationship with Beth to an end but I still thought about her all the time. "I'm not doing any arguing. I'm done with that part. I just want to hear her voice and ask how her mom, Mrs. Frankie, is doing. And will you please stop smacking in my ear!"

Shorty Brown laughs and says, "Me and Rhonda went to Blue Front BBQ and these ribs are bangin'."

"The sweet potato pie is too, Helimite!" Rhonda yells out in the background.

"Y'all make sure to take some pictures for me tonight and send them soon not later. I'm trying to fill up my photo album." The pictures take me to another part of the world that's not surrounded by razor wire and gun towers. To actually see my friends and family smiling and having a good time makes me yearn for free society.

Shorty Brown answers, "Child please! All the pictures me and Rhonda and Beth sent you last year. It should already be full."

"That album is full," I respond. "I have a brand new one I'm working on."

"Oh okay. Are you still at Polk C.I. with Ant and Freddie Jay?" she asks.

"Nope," I answer, "I got transferred to a new prison. Let me talk to Rhonda before you call Beth on three-way."

She hands the phone to Rhonda. "What's up Helimite!"

"Rhonda, I might need your help in a few weeks."

"With what?" Rhonda asks.

"I'm gonna try to get Beth to come visit me but I don't want her to drive five hours up here alone. I'll pay for all the expenses."

Rhonda does about six seconds worth of smacking on her food before she answers. "If I don't have anything going on, I'll come. Why you didn't ask Shorty Brown?"

"Because she don't love me like you love me, sis," I say.

"Whatever, Helimite! Let me know the date ahead of time and I'll decide from there." I can clearly see Rhonda rolling her eyes at the thought of driving five hours to visit me at this prison.

"Okay Rhonda! I will," I tell her.

Shorty Brown gets back on the phone and calls Beth on three-way. Beth answers the phone on the second ring. "Hello," she says.

"How you doing, Sassy Red," I say in my Barry White voice.

She takes a deep breath and says, "I'm fine."

The last time I spoke to Beth was at Polk C.I. when she came to visit me on my birthday. Since then she had stopped writing me and I believe that old saying 'Out of Sight, Out of Mind' strongly applies to our situation.

"How's your mom doing?" I ask.

"Momma doing well also."

I can imagine Beth with her hand on her hip and a scowl on her face due to the numerous letters I mailed her complaining about her lack of communication with me. "If at all possible, Beth, I would like to see you next month."

"What prison you at?" she asks.

"Hardee C.I."

I hear her sigh before she asks, "How many hours is it from Palm Beach County?"

"Five hours," I say. "I already talked to Rhonda about riding with you. I will pay for everything."

"I'm not making any promises, Helimite! I have a boyfriend!" Beth snaps back.

"Yes, I know. I have someone I'm talking to as well," I respond. "But I still care about you and your wellbeing."

"You can't care about me if you don't care about my child."

"I never said I had a problem with your child. I said you should have been on birth control or made your boyfriend use a condom."

"At this point, all of that is irrelevant. You need to grow up and realize my life didn't stop because you decided to go to prison. Take care of yourself. If or when I decide to visit you, I'll write you and let you know the date. Until then, don't call me anymore. If your intent is on trying to make me feel guilty about my child..."

"You have sixty seconds remaining on this call." The operator recording announces.

I remained quiet for at least thirty of those sixty seconds. I wanted to tell her that I still loved her but I wasn't about to give her that moment of endearment. "Have fun at Club La Riviera tonight, Beth."

The last thing I heard her say was, "I sure will."

I hang up the phone and went back up the stairs to my cell and did two hundred pushups on my knuckles. I took a shower and began to read this new book I ordered by *Donald Goines* called, *Street Players*. *Donald Goines* had a writing style that placed you inside the book as a character and not a reader and that's just what I needed. I read until my eyes grew tired and fell asleep.

22

As Christmas Eve turned into Christmas morning, I skipped breakfast on purpose and rolled out of bed at 9:00 a.m. to the sounds of *Kurtis Blow Christmas Rappin'* on my radio. I got dressed, went out the door. It was a beautiful Christmas morning. Everybody was outside in different huddles with their homeboys chillin'. I stopped by the canteen to buy an orange juice and this brother named J.B. was in line behind me. He asked me if I wanted to buy some weed. I told him, "Nope." This was just a stunt to inform me that he was selling a little something but he had his chest poked out like he had a few pounds of weed.

He goes on to say, "Anybody selling any powder out here? Christmas ain't Christmas without no snow."

That's the second time I've heard that in two days. I told him, "Maybe so. What you trying to get? A 8-ball?"

"Yeah. If it's available," J.B. answers.

I whisper, "I got two grams for sale for $200."

He asks, "Is it fire?"

"Yes," I answer. "South Florida Finest. Dade County special. Follow me to the Barber Shop."

We step into the Barber Shop. I speak to my barber then turn my back to him and everyone else except J.B. I reach into my pocket and hand him the powder cocaine that Hollywood had given me the day before. I was going to take it to Medical and hide it up there to get it out of my cell but J.B. seemed to be right on time. He told me he wanted it but didn't have the cash on him. I told him to get it to me later and I walked off. I knew J.B. worked for Black Jack hustling weed and rock so I wasn't worried about getting my money. I'll give a hustler some credit before I will a non-hustler. Today was Christmas but I wasn't giving away anything.

I walked with a pep in my step down that long sidewalk toward the Medical Department. The sun was starting to heat up and I had no plans on being in the heat much longer. Once I entered Medical, it was plain to see that they were short-staffed due to the holiday. The officer who let me in wasn't even a certified officer. She was a trainee. She wouldn't be a problem at all. She actually told me, "Merry Christmas," and went right back to her crossword puzzle.

Once I entered the main hallway, Nurse Brooks came out of medical records with a file in her hand and spoke to me. "Merry Christmas, Helimite."

I respond, "Merry Christmas, Nurse Brooks." She had a beautiful personality. She was in her 60's and had a special love for horses. She had pictures of horses all over her office desk.

"Do you need anything, Nurse Brooks?" I ask.

"No. I'm okay. Thank you," she answers.

"Are you the only nurse here today?"

She replies, "No. Nurse Precious went to confinement to drop off some medication."

I respond, "Yes ma'am," and head to the back where my stash spot is located. I take an empty mop bucket and turn it upside down to use for extra height. I lift up the ceiling panel and grab two ounces and come back down. Timing was everything when it came to my stash spot.

I reach for a garbage bag to roll the two ounces up in to keep the smell down. I walk down the hall to that empty isolation cell that Duck and I had turned into our hiding spot whenever we were caught up with our work. I push the door open and to my surprise, Duck is already back here hiding.

"Merry Christmas, brother," Duck says.

I respond, "Likewise my brother."

Duck says, "With New Year's right around the corner, it's good to know that this year is almost done with."

"Yea. I know that's right," I chime in.

Duck asks, "Helimite, I have my lady coming to visit me today. She should be here within the hour. Did you get a chance to talk to your people about the two ounces?"

"Yeah," I say, "I spoke with them and they said to fix your money."

"My money don't need fixing, Helimite, because I'm never broke."

"I hear you, Duck." I hand him the trash bag.

He says, "I took out all the trash in the building already."

I say, "It's two ounces inside the bag." He unrolls it, smells the ounces, goes to his sock and hands me some bills. I count it in front of him. There are ten one-hundred-dollar bills. "Alright Duck. We good."

He puts the two ounces inside of a knee brace he has on and leaves. I sit there for about thirty minutes before I hit the hallway again. It's empty and quiet in Medical. I turn down another hallway and enter Nurse Precious 27's office. She looks up, startled at first. "Well, Merry Christmas, Helimite."

"Merry Christmas, Precious. Where my gift at?" I say.

"I'm so sorry, Helimite. I didn't know I was required to get something for you," Nurse Precious 27 teases.

"It isn't required but would have been nice. Can I at least get a hug?" I ask.

"Yes, you can, my teddy bear." She rises to meet me.

As I hug Precious, my hands wander all over her ass, lifting and squeezing. I go inside my pocket and peel off two one-hundred-dollar bills and say, "Merry Christmas my Precious friend."

She was caught off guard and speechless. Her first words were, "Where did you get this money from?"

"That's too much information, Precious. That's my gift to you so don't investigate it."

She is looking like she wants to cry. She hugs me again and says, "Thank you," but this time allowing me to tongue kiss her. When we break from kissing she says, "I really wish I could take you home with me."

And I respond, "I really wish you could too."

"Helimite," she begins. "You really don't know what you're getting yourself into. There's a fire and desire inside of me that is very passionate. Have you ever been intimate with a Latin woman?"

"No. I haven't but I'm looking forward to it," I say.

"Well, it is a delicious experience, Helimite, especially with me!" She sticks her tongue out at me and giggles.

I really like the way she says 'delicious'. I hadn't heard that expression before pertaining to sex or lovemaking. I look at my *Guess* watch. It's 11:20 a.m. Count time is at 11:45 so I need to gather some cleaning material and head back to the lobby and look extremely busy. I tell Precious not to leave the prison for lunch at noon but to tell Nurse Brooks that you were leaving. That way, Nurse Brooks wouldn't expect to see you anymore until at least 1:00 p.m.

Nurse Precious asks me why and what for and I tell her to trust me and that I have something important to show her. She agrees and I hurry to the Medical Lobby and begin to clean the floors and benches. At 11:45, the officer who had finally put her crossword puzzle down asks me if I was the only orderly left in the building. I tell her yes and then she asks me for my dorm and room number. I give it to her and continue to clean for five more minutes. The Medical

Officer calls in her count. I go back inside Medical and put away my cleaning supplies.

I make my way back to Nurse Precious 27's office. I tell her to turn off the light and close the door and follow me. I quietly lead her to the X-ray Room. It's locked. I take my I.D. badge and pick the door's lock. In two seconds flat, we enter the room and gently close the door. The X-ray Room is huge with beige walls filled with charts. A fluorescent light hangs from the center of the room and is the only source of light as there aren't any windows. The x-ray machine is against the wall to the left. The room features a cushioned table in the center and there's a dark room in the back to the right.

"So, this is what you wanted to show me?" She asks.

"No," I respond and I pull out my manhood out that is at full attention.

She reaches out to stroke it as I begin to tongue kiss her passionately. She looks me in the eyes and says, "You want pussy or you want head?"

I tell her, "We have at least one hour. I want both so I can decide if everything is delicious or not."

She sits in a nearby chair and pulls me to her and begins sucking and licking my balls, asking me in between breaths, "Do you like this, papi?"

"Hell yeah. Keep doing what you doing, Precious," I whisper. She grabs my manhood and begins to slap herself in the face with it and against her tongue then she engulfs me in her mouth. It was warm and dry at first until she begins to gag from me being in her throat. Her mouth becomes wetter and at times even sloppy wet. She grabs my balls with one hand and concentrates on sucking and deep throating me trying to make me explode.

I pull my manhood out of her mouth because I knew I was about to release. She eagerly asks me, "What's wrong?"

I stare into her eyes while pulling my pants up and while adjusting my hard-on at the same time, "Wait here. I need to check something."

I ease out the door, grab a broom like I am sweeping the hallway. I enter an office with a window and look through the blinds and see inmates in line waiting to eat, which tells me that count has officially cleared. I was so caught up in the moment I didn't know if count had cleared or if there was a recount in progress, which would have meant an officer would be searching high and low for me.

I go back to the X-ray Room and let myself in. Nurse Precious 27 is naked now and reaching for me. I get naked in no time at all.

Nurse Precious 27 asks, "Where the fuck did you go?"

I say nothing to her because I am speechless at how gorgeous this woman's body is.

"I want you to fuck me good. My body is your gift for today."

Nurse Precious 27 begins to strike different poses for me. Her body is a perfect ten in every pose. No scratches, cuts, scars, or stretch marks. Flawless. Her breasts are the size of grapefruits with the prettiest nipples my young eyes had ever seen. I pull her to me and begin to suck on her bottom lip, face, and neck until she forces her tongue into my mouth.

As we share that long, passionate tongue kiss, I pick her up and lay her on her back on the x-ray table with her ass at the very edge. I put both her legs on my shoulder and enter her wetness in one swift motion with both of my feet firmly planted on the floor. Both my hands brace the x-ray table and I stand up in her with a steady stiff stroke, hitting the walls of her vagina.

She places her hands on my biceps as I keep a steady rhythm. All you can hear is flesh slapping against flesh and Nurse Precious 27 saying, "I'm cumming. I'm cumming. Don't stop. Fuck me harder, Helimite!" And fuck her I did. After ten minutes of that position I lay her on her stomach and I pound her from the back while she moans, "Merry Christmas, Helimite. This your pussy!" I explode inside of her still hoping I could fertilize an egg or two.

We are both breathless. Beads of sweat had formed on her back and neck that made her skin glisten under the harsh fluorescent light. Nurse Precious 27 jumps up and searches for her clothes as she realizes the danger in getting caught with an inmate. We quickly gather our clothes and get dressed. I grab my broom again and tell her to wait while I check the hallways and I slide out the door.

When the coast is clear, I lead her out the door and sigh with relief at how smooth we made that happen. Nurse Precious 27 was now comfortable with letting me fuck her every time the opportunity presented itself, which would be often. I really enjoyed the love making on Tuesdays and the straight fucking on Fridays. We always had at least an hour at lunch time to feed our appetites for each other. The way things were going, I really didn't care if Beth came to visit or not. Life was good for me at this time in the prison system and I was seizing the moment. Merry Christmas to me!

23

Nurse Precious 27 was cooking all these good Latin meals for me on a regular basis so I was eating well. She also showed me how to get an outside phone line inside the building. You pick up the phone, push 8 and get a new dial tone to call wherever you want at the State of Florida's expense. I start using the phone in the x-ray room to call everyone but my momma. It would be too much to explain to my momma and she would never agree to me breaking any rules, period.

I call my homeboy Sam and he picks up on the first ring. "Hello."

"Whassup Archie Ball!" (Sam's nickname)

"Helimite, where you at?" Sam asks.

"I'm still locked up in this modern-day plantation."

"I know that but are you back in the Palm Beach County Jail where you can call people for free again?"

"Naw," I answer. "With some help I was able to figure out how to make calls for free up in here where I work."

"Oh okay. Where they got you working at?"

"In the Medical Department."

Sam replies, "That sounds sweet!"

"It is, homeboy! I'm getting my dick wet on a regular basis up in here."

"Is that right? But you never gonna tell how much pussy you eating, Helimite."

I couldn't help but laugh, "I'm gonna leave all that pussy eating to you and Bakebean. Y'all hold the title in Stonybrook for eating pussy." That comment made Sam burst out in laughter. "What's really happening, Sam?"

He answers, "Well, Monica is pregnant and I gotta get two jobs to start saving up for pampers and milk."

"When is she due?" I ask.

"In February."

"Well you have two months to power up. Looks like you should have done more eatin' than skeetin', my brother. You locked in now for 18 more years whether y'all together or not."

"Yeah. You dead right, Helimite, but at this point I'm ready for the responsibility."

"And I salute you for that, Sam. I heard y'all boys riding clean in them *Delta* '88 convertibles right now."

"Yeah, Helimite. Me, Snake, Moochie and Ten. You do know that Ten is dating your soul sister Shorty Brown, right?"

I respond, "Yeah she mentioned it to me the other day when I spoke to her."

Sam continues, "We be taking trips to Atlanta for Freaknik and to the Daytona Spring Break. It be so thick out there."

"I can only imagine, Sam. Y'all need to send me some pictures from them events when y'all go," I say.

"I'll take the camera with me the next time we do that," Sam promises.

"Okay. I gotta go. I'll call you next week."

"Wait a minute, Helimite. I don't know if you heard but my cousin got killed."

"Yeah, I heard about Teddy Donald's death," I say.

"That's old news, Helimite. My other cousin, Fireball, got killed last week. It's so much shooting going on out here. Things are out of control," Sam says.

I respond, "You're absolutely right, Sam. Just keep doing what you do, working and rapping. Continue to stay sucka free and buster free. I need Ten's phone number so I can rap with him 'bout something. He still in Pleasant City getting his hustle on?"

"I believe so but I can't say for sure," Sam replies.

"Do y'all have some good weed in Riviera Beach right now?" I ask.

"Hell yeah," Sam says. In my mind, I see the excitement on his face when he says it.

"What y'all smokin' on?" I ask.

"D. White and Maurice out of Magnolia Park got that fire. They named it 'primo'. It's gas," Sam states!

"Get they number for me. Tell them I asked for it and it shouldn't be a problem."

"Okay. I gotcha."

"I call you next week bro. Later."

The new year was about to come in and I had no New Year's resolution. The life I was living was just fine with me and if anybody else had a problem with the comfort zone I had created for myself, I would handle it by any means necessary. In prison you have to be selfish, for the most part, because of your surroundings. Prison is and will always be cutthroat and the very minute the inmates find a way to get in your business is the day you begin to fall. I was respectfully hated and I embraced my respect and hate.

It was New Year's Day when I finally ran into J.B. again. I asked him about the two hundred dollars he owed me for the cocaine I gave him on Christmas day. He apologized for the delay and asked me for an address where he would have his brother mail a money order to. I gave him my sister's address and walked off. I really hope J.B. isn't trying to size me up 'bout my money.

J.B. was around 6'1", 230 pounds. He played a lot of basketball and swore he was good but, truth be told, he was just average on the court. Basketball is a game of hustle. If you're not prepared to run up and down that court continuously you are in the way.

The riot that took place on the basketball court had been squashed. The Muslim community came to me and Jolly and asked us to do away with our differences, to keep the peace between Palm Beach County, Broward County and Miami Dade County. We all normally got along just fine until that one isolated incident happened. To seal the peace treaty, Jolly met me out in the middle of the softball field with a joint of some Miami weed that he called Judah. I had a joint of that Kryptonite weed. We sat down in the grass like the Native Americans did back in the old days. Instead of passing a peace pipe around, we passed joints back and forth and talked about sports with everybody on the Rec Yard watching closely to make sure our meeting didn't turn violent.

I still refused to play any sports. I continued to stack my paper and fuck Nurse Precious 27. She had to be pregnant by now as much as I was dropping loads of sperm in her. It never occurred to me that she just might be on birth control.

24

Time was standing still for no one. It is now February and the prison administration planned special programs specifically for Black History Month. Different church organizations, outreach groups, and motivational speakers, were scheduled to come in and do services. Lieutenant Laws had a DJ from the local radio station 102JAMZ come in. He set up shop on the basketball court with all his music equipment to host a Black History Month talent show.

The day of the talent show was a beautiful day to be outside. 72 degrees and overcast. They placed caution tape around all the music equipment so the DJ had space. The talent show would start at 1:00 p.m. and end at 3:30 p.m. When the 12-noon count cleared and the yard opened up for everybody to eat lunch, all you heard was bass from rap and R&B music being played loud and clear on the prison yard. The winner of the talent show would get fifty dollars in canteen for food or hygiene products.

Every Black staff member from every department was on hand to support every program event that was on the calendar. The DJ was setting the tone for a laid-back afternoon. He had *Naughty By Nature*'s hit song, *Hip Hop Hooray* bumping and I could see the Black female staff trying not to dance because they were at work. The DJ put on *Xscape*'s, *Just Kickin It* next. As I watched the crowd grow, everybody present was singing along.

Nardo walks up, gives me a fist bump and says, "This thing thick like Gaines Park on a Sunday in West Palm Beach."

I respond, "Hell yeah." I ask Nardo, "Where Dr. Rock?" Nardo said that Dr. Rock was probably still at work.

"Nardo, look at how tight Sgt. Carter pants is."

"Yeah Helimite. I don't know how she got into them pants this morning."

"And it look like she wearing her daughter's panties today," I say. "Look at all that booty. She sho got something to sit on."

Nardo nods his head in agreement.

It's 12:50 p.m. and the talent show would start soon.

"Let's go to the store to get something to drink, Nardo."

We walk over toward the store. I look to my right and guess who I see? J.B. with a nice gold chain on with a V-neck shirt, some blue shorts on and brand-new blue and white Nikes on his feet. I buy three Sprites, give Nardo one and walk over to J.B. who is talking to his boss man, Black Jack.

"What up y'all," I hand J.B. a sprite and say, "Let me speak to you a minute brother."

He walks off with me and asks, "Your sister got that two hundred my brother sent, right?"

I said, "No. She didn't!"

"What!" he says, raising his voice. "My brother don't play 'bout no money, Helimite."

"And I don't either, J.B. You been owing me for almost two months now."

J.B. gets loud again, "Man stop sweatin' me about them two hundred dollars. My brother say he sent it."

I respond, "J.B. your brother don't owe me. You do!"

"Just tell your sister to keep checkin' the mail," and he walks off with his chest all poked out like he was the big dog on the yard.

I go back to where Nardo is standing and explain to him the game J.B. been playing for almost two months now. Nardo is listening and weighing the situation out to provide me with a common-sense response. "You shouldn't have credit him nothing you couldn't stand to take a loss on."

I respond, "Nardo, our word is all we have in prison and that negro gonna pay me or I'm gonna beat his ass."

"When?" Nardo asks.

"The first chance I get. Tomorrow!"

"Wait 'til after Black History Month over with first, Helimite."

I look Nardo in the eyes and say, "It could be Yellow history month. I'm gonna beat dude up tomorrow! I'm not asking you to help me but I do need you to watch my back and make sure nobody jumps in to try and save him."

"I'm gonna watch your back but if you go to confinement I'm not sending nothing back there to you to read, eat, or smoke."

"That's fine with me, homeboy," I say.

The talent show had started and there was a brother up there trying to sing a *Luther Vandross* song, *A House Is Not A Home*. The inmates boo'd his ass off the stage. The next contestant did a stand-up routine that was good and then these two damn fools, Funk Master and M.T. got up there and did some freestyle dancing to the song *Playing At Your Own Risk*. That really had the crowd turnt up with laughter. This was the first time I had ever seen Hardee C.I. this care free and laid-back. The inmates were really looking forward to all the scheduled events on the calendar for the rest of February.

I was deep in thought, half listening to some brother do the *MLK I Have a Dream* speech. If I am to follow through with beating J.B.'s ass tomorrow, I didn't really want to cause such a disturbance that security locks the prison down and cancels any of the programs that are scheduled. With that in mind, I started moving around through the crowd finding my most loyal, straight up goons. I explained to five of them that I needed them to meet with me in the morning at 8:30 a.m. and to come packing with a weapon. That gave me a six-man safety net to redirect traffic and to discourage any of J.B.'s fan club from intervening.

With all that groundwork done, I was just in time to hear Normskee, the confinement orderly, and his homeboy Sir Crown do a rap song titled *When the Cats Away the Mouse Will Play*. I must admit that these two brothers were on point with their rhymes and the hook stole the crowd for sure. They would go on to win the fifty-dollar prize. Normskee really did bless the mic and the compound with his talents today.

The yard is being called for 4:00 p.m. count. "All inmates, report to your dorms immediately."

As the crowd of inmates are making their way to their dorms the last song being played was *The Gap Band's* hit song *Outstanding*. The DJ's name was JoMomma Johnson. He had brought peace and harmony to one of the most violent prisons in Florida, Hardee C.I. I went back to my dorm and decided I wasn't going to dinner or back on the compound for third yard. I had three boiled eggs, an onion, and a tomato. I would fix my world-famous tuna salad. I open a box of club house crackers and listen to my radio. I might write somebody and smoke me a joint. How can I forget that? It's easy to forget when you high all the time, I guess, but this too shall pass. Trust me. All with time. I'm full and I'm high and *Frankie Beverly* and *Maze* are singing about *We Are One*.

I close my eyes to take that trip back down memory lane. Remembering it all is one of my favorite things to do. The West Palm Beach Auditorium was so packed for the *New Edition, Force MDs,* and *Cherelle* concert. It was hard trying to find any parking. I only lived, at the most, a mile away from the auditorium on 13th Street behind Gaines Park.

I had gone to the Palm Beach Mall earlier that day to get a fresh outfit to wear. I picked up a pair of black *Adidas* shoes, white *Lee* jeans and a black *Polo* shirt with a white fur *Kangol*. I sprayed on my *Drakkar* cologne and hit the door.

I called Nicole earlier that day to see if she was still going to the concert and she responded, "Yes." I told her to meet me by the photo booth at 10 p.m. She agreed and I hung up. Since this was officially a slow jam concert, I decided not to roll with the Stonybrook crew because I felt like it wouldn't be a good look at a slow jam concert. I went by myself until I hit the parking lot and bumped into one of my classmates named Aldric. He was *Polo* clean as well as all North Shore Mustangs were known for back then.

I give Aldric a hand slap and say, "It's wall to wall up in there, Aldric."

He nods in agreement and says, "At least twenty females to every guy, for sure, Helimite!"

"I hope so," I say.

We climb the mountain of stairs and produce our tickets at the ticket booth and began a slow walk around the auditorium, looking and bobbing our heads to the song *Roxanne Roxanne*. Fans had driven from as far as Miami to watch this concert and the mood inside this building felt so right. There were bodies of all shapes and sizes there with a variety of colors on as well.

The first singer to take stage was my baby *Cherrelle* and when she finally sang her hit with *Alexander Oneil, Saturday Love*, the night and tempo had been set. She left the stage with a thunderous applause and ovation from the crowd. I go to get me a cold drink. Aldric was still rolling with me, getting phone numbers as we moved through the crowd. Rule number one, at any concert back then, was bring your own pen and paper. I check my watch and it was five minutes 'til 10 p.m. I had to meet up with Nicole if I wanted to see her when this concert was over with tonight.

I ordered two large cokes and a large popcorn. When Nicole showed up, I saw her before she saw me and I must say that she was wearing that pink *Fila* sweat suit well. All eyes were on her so I stepped up and made myself seen. I hand her a coke and the popcorn. She thanks me, hugs me, and goes to the restroom with some other females from Twin Lakes High School. When she returns, I am already in the photo line. She joins me and we take four pictures together at five dollars a piece. I let her keep two and we talked briefly about meeting up at Denny's afterward and then we went our separate ways.

Aldric said, "Damn, Helimite. That's your girl?"

"Not yet," I laughed. "But I'm working on it.

He laughed and said, "I bet!"

The group *Force MD's* was on stage next and the song everybody was waiting on was *Tender Love* and when they sang it, they delivered it pretty well. Last but not least, *New Edition* closed things out and they showed their asses off with their performance. Me and Aldric were in between an army of females hollering and screaming, "Ronnie, Bobby, Ricky, Mike, Ralph!"

I overheard one guy tell his girl, "Let's see if *New Edition* gonna give yo ass a ride back to Miami. Now act like you got a man and some sense." We laughed hard at that.

I didn't know which girl it was but somebody kept grabbing the little ass I had in my *Lee* jeans and all I wanted to do was grab back. The lights went down way low and *New Edition* asked everyone in the auditorium to join hands even if you don't know the person next to you. I step back some to align my hand-holding with some females. I wasn't holding Aldric's hand and I'm sure he felt the same way.

New Edition sang *Lost In Love* and the women couldn't stop crying. I'm like, "Damn. I need to learn how to sing instead of rap." These young women really loved *New Edition* and it was written all over their faces. Once that song ended the concert ended and me and Aldric pushed and squeezed our way to the right exit closest to our vehicles.

As we came down the mountain of steps, my mind was racing with thoughts of hanging out with Nicole later at Denny's. It was so crowded I never even recognized the entourage of guys headed directly toward me until it was too late. I got pushed in the chest hard and a voice shouted, "Where all your partners at now bitch boy?" I gathered myself and took notice of who was talking to me and who was now surrounding me. All I could do was pray it didn't turn out too bad.

I immediately hollered out, "It take all y'all to beat me up Hotdog? Fight me head up and let's see who come out on top." This request caught Hotdog completely off guard. I was only 5'10", maybe 165 back then but trust me when I say I came up fighting and knew how to throw hands and wrestle. Hotdog was all fresh out of jail, swol' up, and had his crew scared of him. Wherever Aldric went, I hope he got back ASAP with some help. Aldric wasn't about this life and I didn't expect him to even try to have my back in this spot.

I looked to my left and saw my classmate Kay Kay watching it all about to play out. If I'm not mistaken, she was dating Hotdog at the time. Hotdog yelled out, "I got this y'all," and tried to bum rush me. I served him with a two piece to his head. Because I was so skinny, Hotdog wanted to get his hands on me to try and wrestle me down but I decided to take the wrestle game to him instead and scooped him off his feet with his back landing at the very front of the flight of stairs headed into the auditorium. I had a lock on him that he couldn't wiggle out of. With all the strength I had in me, I lift him off the ground and try to throw him over a railing that was at least a ten-foot drop and had about two feet of water at the bottom. This clearly would have ended his life due to all the colorful light bulbs in the two feet of water that would have burst on Hotdog's impact and electrocuted him.

His crew wasn't having any of that. I was bum rushed by at least six dudes who proceeded to beat my ass up, blow after blow after blow. I guess that still wasn't satisfaction enough for them because they tried to throw me over that same railing to my death but I called on Jesus and held on to the railing like some *Gorilla* glue. All of a sudden two ladies ran over to us and began screaming and hollering for the police. Hotdog and his crew fled.

I sat on the ground for at least twenty minutes, punch drunk. My head and body ached something terrible. For one, I was so disappointed that I decided, earlier in the evening, against carrying my .380 pistol to this slow jam concert. Two, I was disappointed that I chose not to go to the concert with the Stonybrook crew. I never really thought all the wanna-be thugs and gangsters would attend a slow jam concert but apparently, I was dead wrong and had quite a few knots and a couple of broken ribs to show for my bad decision-making.

"Hey Helimite. You alright?"

I look up and it's Aldric. I nod my head yes and get up and stumble through the parking lot to my car and drive home. When I walk through the door, I was grateful everyone was asleep. I went to the bathroom, looked in the mirror and cursed under my breath, "No matter what the cost, Hotdog is going to die before the week is out."

25

I wake up the next morning to the smell of rain. It is a slow and steady drizzle at Hardee C.I., no thunder or lightning, which was the perfect setting to beat some sense into J.B.'s head. I leave my room and go to the mop room that's wide open for anybody needing a broom or mop. I close the door and take out my finger nail clipper. I use the back end that I had filed down to use as a screw driver. I reach up and start unscrewing the mop closet vent cover. I stand on a turned over mop bucket to be able to reach deep inside that vent to pull free my solid steel pipe almost similar to the one I had at Polk C.I.

I sit the pipe on the floor, put the vent back and put my pipe inside my pant leg. Once I get to my room, I put on my 2X jacket that didn't seem out of place due to the rain. I slide my pipe up the right sleeve and walk out the door to meet with my guys and brief them on the target. Nobody knew I had a pipe on me, not even Nardo and we're like family. Because of the rain, all of the inmates have hats and jackets on. The best part about it is that security would be ducking the rain all day. They weren't getting paid enough to get soaking wet.

I am posted up by the bleachers when I see J.B. and two of his homeboys come out of the dorm. They're talking loud about who was the best NBA player out of Michael Jordan and Magic Johnson. I come from behind the bleacher and put my back up against the wall, in front of the Barber Shop. As soon as J.B. turned the corner, I let my pipe slide down to my hand and strike J.B. between his shoulder blade. He grunts in deep pain sounding like a pig as I grab him by the back of his neck and snatch his gold chain. I strike him two more times landing blows on his forearm, that I'm sure is broken, and another blow across his back. He tries to flee. His two homeboys had been yoked out and removed from the set. I slid my pipe back up my sleeve, pulled my hat down, and walked slowly back to my dorm to replace my pipe inside the vent.

I played sick and stayed in the dorm the rest of the day playing poker. J.B.'s boss man, Black Jack stepped to me to ask me what was going on with me and J.B. I told him the truth that J.B. owed me two hundred dollars for almost two months so I went and got paid.

Black Jack asks me, "What's it gonna cost to get the gold chain back?"

I answer, "Four hundred dollars."

He asks for an address and I told him to have the money sent to my prison account. Two days later, at mail call, I was handed a blue envelope with a bald eagle on the outside. Inside the envelope was a receipt that said that four hundred dollars was deposited to my inmate account. I gave Black Jack the gold chain and he responded, "Please don't ever credit J.B. anything else."

I said, "I doubt he will ever want any more credit."

The following day the brother 36 from Miami was waiting for me outside my dorm. "Hey Helimite. Let me rap with you for a minute."

"What's on your mind, 36?"

"I got escorted to the Security Building last night and this female inspector was up there questioning me and some other inmates about some weed and two knives they found inside the water fountain. She feel like since my room by the water fountain I got to know something so she asked me who E-mite was. I told her I never heard of no E-mite. She said,

281

'you know who he is. He's controlling this compound with officers on his payroll but it's all coming to an end here shortly.'"

I look at 36 and say, "Well whoever E-mite is, he better tighten his game up."

36 returns my stare and says, "Dog, you gotta know that the inspector is referring to you but got your name wrong but close to it."

I nod my head and say, "It is what it is. Let's see how the cards fall, 36." I give him a hand slap and head on up to Medical. There are ten officers there and a dog in the lobby. They ask me to have a seat in the lobby then took me in the inmate restroom and had me strip down naked.

"What y'all lookin' for, Officer?" I ask.

The officer answers, "Anything illegal, Helimite."

"Okay, sir. Nothing from nothing leaves nothing and that's all I have besides these 55 years."

"Just sit down and shut the fuck up, Helimite."

I look at the officer and make a mental note to reach out and touch him in the next riot. The next thing I know, they're telling me to cuff up.

"For what?" I ask.

"Because we gave you a direct order to, inmate!"

I turn around and cuff up. They take me to the captain's office and when I walk in, Duck is in the hallway in handcuffs and Inmate Gene is coming out of the inspector's office in handcuffs. I look at Duck like, "Whassup?" He shrugs his shoulders and stays quiet. When my turn comes to be questioned the female inspector claims to have found over 36 grams worth of weed. She claims her officer found it inside the Medical Department and asks me what I knew about it and was it mine.

I look her right in the face and say, "I never knew they had weed in prison."

She looks at me and says, "Yeah, right. You're just an innocent Christian guy in prison for jay-walking, right? I received your file from Polk C.I. You're no stranger to the illegal hustles that go on inside the prisons and you most definitely play your part in it."

She barks out an order, "Lock him up under investigation and keep him separated from the other two medical orderlies."

"10-4," the officer responds and escorts me out of the room.

Now Duck or Inmate Gene must have hidden that weed in the building and didn't do a good job of it and were refusing to tell on themselves because there was enough weed to get an outside charge and have more years added on to their sentence. I'm hot as fish grease, of course, but what can I do? I'm under investigation, which could last up to six months if the inspector wanted to be nasty and this dyke-looking inspector was going to drag us back here.

Two months had passed. I had a cell by myself, plenty of food and my radio was with me. I had a routine I stuck with to pass every day away. I had been writing letters but no one seemed to be writing me back. On May 15, 1993, after three months of being in confinement, under investigation, I received four letters. My momma and my homeboys Bug, Bowly, and Chik. When I open the letter from my momma it was dated March 26, 1993.

My Son,

May the Lord watch between you and me while we are absent one from another. I know people use this as a benediction but I need my Father who art in heaven to watch over my son. It seems you and trouble keep running into one another. I was very honored to receive all your cards. So sorry to hear of your confinement status. I trust it is about over. You never have to concern yourself about my praying for you. I do that daily. I just pray you too are praying.

The Bible declares that one can chase one thousand demons away and two people praying can put ten thousand demons to flight but it must be effective, fervent prayer. Myself and Pastor Gladys are trusting that God will move on your behalf.

Read scriptures Luke 18:1 and Isaiah 2:6-7 and Col 4:2, son. Please ask the Lord to help you to follow him and let His will be done in your life. You are not forgotten. I miss and love you, my son. Write your sisters. They need to hear from you, Son. Get in God's presence.

Love Your Mom,

Dot Jones

"I love you too momma," I say to myself as I sit on my bunk and read the letter again. I realized that security had been withholding my mail. My momma wrote this almost a month and a half ago and the letter from Bug, Bowly and Chik was a month old as well. I was extremely hot now. What if one of my family members was in the hospital or there was a death in the family. This investigation shit had been going on too long now. I grab a pen and an inmate request form. I check the box that said 'inspector' and begin to write.

Inspector Patterson,

I respect that you have a job to do but the only way you can complete a puzzle is with all the pieces. Can you please come talk with me when your schedule permits?

I turned that request form in that night. Two days later I was standing up on the top bunk looking out the window at the parking lot listening to *Let's Chill* by *Guy* when Officers Larison and Beers appear at my cell door. "Inmate Helimite. Get in Class A uniform. You have some people here to see you."

I turn around and say, "People? That's plural. Who is it? I might refuse to go."

"Inspector Patterson and her Boss."

What I didn't know but would find out later on, the minute those two female inspectors hit the parking lot and came through the control room, phone calls were being made that something big was about to go down among the Hardee C.I. staff.

I jump down off the top bunk and begin to get dressed. I grab my lotion bottle that had some *Joop* cologne mixed in it and put some on. They cuff me up, add shackles, and escort me about fifty feet to a conference room that was also used as a disciplinary hearing room.

Officers Larison and Beers made a smart remark saying, "Inmate Helimite, whatever I've done to you in the past, please forgive me. I really need my job."

I look at them, laugh, and say, "Piggly Wiggly grocery store is hiring, dude so relax." As I approach the conference room, Officer Sims looks right at me from the control booth and shakes his head. I've assisted officers with situations that were beyond their reach of control in return for favors, **quiet as kept**. And these same three officers, Sims, Beers, and Larison were all tight as fish pussy and knew I held and kept life-changing information about Hardee C.I.

Beers opens the door. The two female inspectors are seated at the far side of the table with a tape recorder and brand-new legal pads and ink pens in their hands. Inspector Patterson dismisses the two officers and ask them to leave the room and shut the door behind them. The other female inspector was actually the Regional Inspector. She sniffed the air in the conference room and asks, "What's that smell?"

I respond, "Oh. That's me. I smell good everywhere I go. It's a hygiene habit."

"My name is Inspector Queen. You can have a seat," as she points at the seat across her.

"No thank you. I'd rather stand," I say.

Inspector Queen pauses with a surprised look on her face, "Okay then. You sent a request form asking to speak with Inspector Patterson."

"Yes, I did."

"And what is it concerning," she asks as she reaches out to hit the record button on the tape player.

"Yes ma'am. I want to know if you all have a problem with my incoming and outgoing mail."

Both inspectors look at each other and Inspector Patterson asks, "What are you talking about?" as she reaches for a cigarette and lights it up.

I respond, "I haven't received any mail from anyone in over two months until two days ago and those letters were dated and post marked from almost a month ago. I'm not the smartest person in the world but I do know it's a federal offense to hold or tamper with U.S. mail."

The regional inspector Ms. Queen who was a redbone with, what looked like, a pound of makeup on stopped the tape recorder and looked at me and said, "I know you didn't request for us to come here to talk about your mail. I drove almost four hours to get here from Tallahassee."

"With all due respect Ms. Queen…"

"It's Inspector Queen to you, inmate," she interrupts.

"Okay then, Inspector Queen, my mail is important to me. I have been in confinement for over three months under investigation and no one has given me any kind of status check on when this bogus investigation will end."

Inspector Queen says, "It can end today if you cooperate and give us the names of the staff members assisting you in the drug trafficking business you have established at Hardee C.I. I've reviewed your file. We are more than capable of transferring you to a prison closer to your family in West Palm Beach."

"Are you assuring me that you have the power to get me to Glades Correctional Institution in Belle Glade?" I ask.

"Yes, I have that authority," Inspector Queen remarks as she sits back into her chair and fidgets with the pen in her hand.

"Well, if you have that much power you can stop these clowns from withholding my mail at this prison," I scold.

Inspector Queen fires back, "I don't work for the Post Office, Inmate Helimite. I work for the Inspector General's Office."

I nod my head and respond, "It's two thing I never did like, Inspector Queen. A silly ass dog that chases cars and a redbone with a whole bunch of make up on."

Inspector Patterson bangs down on the conference table while shouting, "You don't talk to a Regional Inspector like that, inmate."

Inspector Queen raises her hand to quiet Inspector Patterson and says to me, "I'm gonna send your ass to a prison so far away from Palm Beach County it's gonna make your head spin."

I respond, "I can do time on the moon so your threats don't phase me."

Both inspectors sit silent for a moment and stare at me. "Inmate Helimite, you have some nerve."

"No ladies. Y'all have some nerve. No matter what, I'm **still quiet as kept**."

Inspector Patterson jumps up out of her seat and waves to the officers inside their booth to come escort me back to my cell. Officers Beers and Larison rush out of the officer's station booth and removes me from the conference room. While escorting me back to my cell, Beers looks at me and says, "Inmate Helimite I must admit, you have some balls."

I respond, "What are you talking about now Beers?" and before he could answer, Larison says, "We listened to your whole interview with those inspectors. We had the intercom button turned on for the conference room and heard everything."

I respond, "I hope you all enjoyed the show. At least you know now that everybody that goes before these inspectors are not snitching. With that said, you can inform all your fellow officers that their jobs are still intact."

"Open Cell 12, Sims!" Officer Beers speaks into his walkie talkie. My cell door slides open. I forgot to turn my radio off before I left and the song that was playing was by *Chuckii Booker, Game. Why you wanna play your games on me? Why you wanna play?* I broke into a slow two-step dance with shackles still on my feet. I stood still long enough for the shackles to be removed and then my cell door is shut. I stick my hands through the door slot for my handcuffs to be removed.

I fall back on my bunk and sing along to the song and think about the last two ounces that were still in the ceiling in Medical and shake my head. I guess I have to charge that to the game. At mail call several hours later, I received two letters. One from Barbette and another letter from some unknown person. The front of the envelope said, "Guess Who" with no return address.

Dear Helimite,

It's been way too long since I've talked to you and seen you. A day doesn't go by that I don't think about the times we shared. Things have gotten a lil crazy at this end and I may come to visit you more sooner than later, on a regular basis. Keep your head up and if you ever feel like nobody loves you, remember that I do.

Your Girl Always,

The Real One

I read the letter again and smell the paper. It was sprayed with Ms. Washington's signature perfume scent, that tropical fruit smell. As I dissected her letter, she was saying that things weren't good at Polk C.I. and she was in the process of transferring to Hardee C.I. Ms. Washington is an officer and could never be added to my visitation list so her saying that she will be seeing me on a regular basis could only be as an officer. All I could do was say, "Damn," and shake my head. My girl was coming and I was leaving. She didn't put a return address on the envelope so she will find out I'm gone once they hire her on.

I'm shaking my head now. When it rains, it pours. I get up on my feet, pace back and forth in my cell for an hour, I do two hundred pushups, take a bath in my sink, brush my teeth and crash for the night. The next morning, I awaken to my food slot being opened. I thought it was my breakfast tray but it wasn't. It was the midnight officer advising me that I was transferring this morning and he had some paperwork for me to sign.

I must have really pissed off Inspector Queen to be transferring the very next day. I guess she's showing me how much pull she really has. By the time I am shackled and handcuffed for my trip, it is 8:00 a.m. I see Officer Sims, I call him over to me and say, "Sims, where they transferring me to? Is it north or south?"

He looks at me and says, "Helimite, it's north. Way north. Calhoun Correctional Institution up by Tallahassee."

"Well I'm pretty sure it's cold up there. Good thing I have my jacket with me."

"Take care of yourself, Helimite and concentrate on going home. Growing old in here isn't the life I'm sure you're interested in."

I respond, "No, I'm not, Officer Sims but at the moment I'm kinda stuck in here for 55 years so it is what it is. I'll survive and I'll be **still quiet as kept** through it all.

To be continued....

Ed "Jelly" Harper
No matter what the season, you were always the voice of
reason.
R.I.P. Soul Brother

To My Readers:

I really appreciate everyone who read book one and pushed me, reminded me and aggravated me into finishing book two. Y'all do realize I build power lines for a living so I operate a crane 10-12 hours a day, six days a week so my ass be tired. LOL ☺ I have 17 more books to go so give me a minute. It's gonna happen once again. I appreciate y'all support. The next book is titled, RESPECTFULLY HATED. Until next time, continue to live, love, laugh.

Helimite

www.ingramcontent.com/pod-product-compliance
Lightning Source LLC
Chambersburg PA
CBHW030344020726
47493CB00003B/678